How Did I Get in This Mess?

Doris Greenlee

PublishAmerica
Baltimore

ISBN: 1-60441-626-2
PUBLISHED BY PUBLISHAMERICA, LLLP
www.publishamerica.com
Baltimore

Printed in the United States of America

Dedicated to all my "sister girlfriends"
who have or are on their way to
finding themselves.

First, I would like to thank my Father in heaven for my creation and for placing me in my space in life. I would also like to thank my earthly father who had a passion for the written word; his poetry was always a pleasure for me to read.

To my wonderful, courageous, and strong mother who taught me and is still teaching me even though she is gone, how to "stand" as a woman.

Thanks to all my family; my children Carmen, Bryan and Erica and my sisters and brothers who supported me and cheered me on. To all the other writers in my family, Jerry, Bryan, Lisa; as you always say, Jerry, "It's in the DNA." To my "girls" Charlene, Maxine and Hazel, it's been great; we have shared our hopes, dreams, ups and downs, cried, prayed and played together. Let's keep that up huh?

Last but not least, to everybody that asked me "How's that book coming along? When is it going to be published?" Well, here it is…

Chapter 1

How did I get in this mess? How did you get in this mess, Carol Rice Moneymaker? I've lived forty-four years and what have I learned? What I've discovered is, the longer you live, the more you learn. You say you won't make that mistake again, but, when the opportunity arises, you jump right back into the same mess that it took all your courage, faith, and strength to get out of before.

I haven't been out in months; I think I will be a little adventurous and get out of the house, get my best friend Charlotte to go out with me. Maybe to that jazz club we found out about a few weeks ago.

"Where did he come from? Boy, is he good-looking." So tall and handsome, very mysterious looking, I should really know better. But I am so lonely and feeling so very weak, needing to feel a man's arms around me, it's been so long. I have a man, but he's over five hundred miles away; might as well be on the other side of the world. He has not been very attentive lately; a phone call every now and then, a letter a couple of times a month. I had not seen him in months; he was content to let me do all the work in this relationship. I tried to hold on to us, to keep things going between us. After a while, it seemed as if I was the only one doing all the calling, writing, sending of cards and all the visits to Ohio to see him. I held on for two years, trying to cling to a love that seemed to come out of a dream.

David, the love of my life; I had not seen him for almost nineteen years. He is my soul mate. Have you ever had a soul mate? One of those relationships with a man that will make you so weak that you are willing to do any and everything to be with him? Oh, what a feeling! So tender and pure, so natural, it's like you know you belong together. He is the father of my firstborn, my high school sweetheart. My first, I was a virgin when I met him, so naïve, I didn't know one thing about my body, that I was a sexual being, all I knew was what my mother told me all the time while I was growing up. "Don't get into any cars with boys or you will get in trouble." I never knew, exactly, what she was referring to. Anyway, I didn't get into any cars with any boys, just David. I found out a year later what "trouble" meant. He and I connected immediately. I would always tell my girlfriends that I would know who the love of my life would be; they would say "how would you know that?"

"I would just know" would be my reply and I did *"know."* What a wonderful feeling I had when I was with him. We could talk about anything, everything, he was so gentle and kind and so loving. Of course, we had the usual "please baby, please baby, please baby, please" battle. I won that battle for about four months; by that time, I was totally and completely in *love* with that man-child. It did not matter that he had another girlfriend and that they had a baby daughter together.

All I knew was that I loved that man-child. Man-child, because that was what he was. He was a young male with the problems and responsibilities of a man and not really knowing how to handle them.

When we made love for the first time, it was one Christmas Eve, in the back seat of a car that belonged to one of our friends. The junior choir of the church that I belonged to sponsored a dance to raise money for a trip that we wanted to take to sing in Ohio. This was the perfect opportunity for David and I to get together; he had been working on me for months. Talking to me so gently about how it would be if I gave him some. He did not know how little I knew about sex, or my body. I didn't even know that I had a vagina until he put his finger inside of me one night while we were making out; it felt so good! When I had my first orgasm one night while we were making out, I didn't know what that feeling was that moved all over my body I just knew that it felt wonderful. "What was that?" I remember thinking. We would make out whenever we could when he would come to see me at my house, it was kind of hard considering I had seven brothers and sisters, two parents, and an occasional niece running around all over the place. I was content with not going "all the way" with him, kissing and rubbing and touching was just fine with me, but of course, he wanted more.

That Christmas, I gave him just what he wanted but it didn't turn out to be what I expected. Nothing to write home about, just your usual run-of-the-mill lay in the back seat, insert penis and away he pumped kind of thing. I was so afraid, that I really didn't realize what was going on. I didn't know that this was a natural thing that goes on between a male and female. The physical aspects of that night were not very appealing to me at all. However, the next day, when I woke up I felt *him*, I knew every move he was making that morning, even though he was five blocks away from me at his house, I felt him inside of me, not physically, but inside my soul. Oh how I loved him that morning. This love was so deep and so special; he was my soul mate. This is the feeling people talk about when you become one with another person.

Of course, I ended up getting "in trouble" and a year after we graduated, I gave birth to my oldest daughter. He was, by that time, in the Navy and seeing the world. I was at home still working in a dental office and trying to make it. Things started falling apart between us; there was still the other woman in his life and the other daughter. By the time I carried my baby for nine months by myself, going to the doctor by myself, and handling everything by myself, my heart was broken in two. He ran from me, from her, from their daughter and our unborn child. I tried to find the strength to say goodbye to him, to end the pain some how. Our daughter was born in September and he did not see her until that December. Another Christmas, our daughter was three months old and by that time, I had found the strength to want to be out of that relationship. Besides, he had decided to choose her over me. For some reason, he still thought that we could still kick it. "No way," I said. "You've hurt me too much."

"Well then, just one more time, can we be together?" he said.

"No, this is it, you've made your choice." It took him all day to convince me to go with him; he showed up at my house early Christmas morning and spent the entire day with our daughter Camille and me.

9

"Why are you here with me when you have given her an engagement ring for her Christmas present?"

"I don't know," he said. "Please come with me to my brother's apartment so we can be together for the last time."

I thought about it for a long time and I really didn't want to go, but then I said, "Alright, I'll come with you, but let's not take a cab like you want, let's walk." For some reason, I wanted to walk. It had snowed that day and I loved to walk in the snow. So off we went. The apartment was blocks and blocks away, but everybody walked in that town. While on our way, a car spotted us; it was full of girls—guess whose girls?

"Is that you, David?" came a voice from the car.

"Yeah" was all he said. (The beginning of the end.) Before we got to the apartment, the car showed up again, but this time, his fiancée Tonya Hughes was with them. As she got out of the car, I knew that this would be it. (Time to grow up a little.) "Oh shit" was all he could say. There we were, it looked like "showdown at high noon" only, it was "showdown on Christmas Night." David and I were standing on one end of the block and Tonya at the other end of the same block. He went to her; I don't know what was said to him, but she was letting him have it.

All I heard was something about the ring. He came to me. In my eyes, he was reduced to a young boy. "I don't know what to do" was all he could say to me.

"You brought me out here, you're not going to leave me here." My heart was pounding wanting him to become my hero and walk away with me.

He looked helpless as he turned from me and went to her; they exchanged words. Back and forth he went between the two of us, each one of us giving him an ultimatum. "If you leave me out here tonight, you can forget about me and our child," I told him.

He looked at me and then looked down the street at her, and said those famous words all men seem to say when they find their backs against the wall, "Just fuck it." He walked off and left both of us standing on opposite ends of that sidewalk looking at each other. Tonya looked quite victorious and so sure of herself knowing that she had won. As for me, the most incredible feeling started creeping over me. It seemed as if an enormous weight was lifted off of my shoulders; I literally felt it lift up off of my shoulders! I stood there, waiting to burst into tears, but they never came, I never dropped one tear. I just felt relief, relieved that it was over, really over for me, at last.

As I stood there, she came up to me and said, "No fucking tonight," she got back in the car and her and her girls drove off. I didn't even care about that, I was just glad that it was all over. Now I was out on that street all alone, at night in the cold and had to figure out how to get back home. I was sure that "the girls" would be waiting for me on the other side of the viaduct that I had to walk under to get back home. What was I going to do? I went to call a taxi at the nearest business I could find but, it being Christmas, they were closed. I decided to just walk home and take my chances, when all of a sudden, my brother in-law pulled up out of nowhere. I wondered if he had seen any of what had happened? He gave me a ride home. If anything was said between us, I don't remember. All I know is that I went home and resumed my life as a single mother. It wasn't very hard; I just kept waiting to feel some hurt, some pain behind losing David. But, it never came; I started breathing and looking towards my future with my daughter Camille. Eventually, I started going out with my friends and met an occasional male, nobody that I was too interested in.

I never really looked at myself as being a good-looking young woman even though other people would make a comment on how pretty I was. I never believed them because I just never saw it. My sisters used to tell me that I was ugly, the ugliest one in the family.

They used to tease me relentlessly about my looks, my grades, everything. I guess, as a result, I didn't think too highly of myself. They used to sing a song called "ugliest one in the family, ugliest one in the family." You see everyone used to rave about how beautiful my older sisters were. Our family had a reputation of being "that family with all those pretty girls" except me, according to my sisters. I didn't carry myself with much pride or self-assurance; I was very insecure about myself. I just could not figure out for the life of me why guys seemed to be attracted to me. Anyway, I just worked and came home, took care of my daughter and, like I said, went out on the weekends sometimes. Then, something terrible happened in my life. One of my sisters, whom I had gotten close to, died suddenly.

Another event in life that forces you to stop and look and say, "What is going on?" My sister supposedly took a gun and shot herself. I was nineteen years old. This was a very devastating blow to my entire family. She was so young and very beautiful. No one knows why she did this; everything about that event is all very blurry and dreamlike. I suppose, when something like that happens, it is dreamlike.

Chapter 2

Everyone in our town thought that we had a lot of money; I suppose that was because of the way the family as a whole carried ourselves. We did not have a lot of money. My mother worked as a maid, we would wear hand-me-downs, she would buy things for us at the rummage sale, or the people she worked for would give her clothes that no longer fit their children. One of my sisters could sew very well and she would make clothes for some of us girls for special occasions. My mom was a maid or a day worker and was employed by at least three families. She had specific days that she would go to each home and work. At the end of the day, she would get paid and would go by the store to buy food for our dinner. She was a very strong and proud woman and I am sure this is how we learned to carry ourselves with such pride regardless of the situation we would find ourselves in. She told us that she did not graduate from high school, but quit school during her eleventh-grade year in order to work to help her family.

My father was an educated man; he worked as an occupational therapist at the local state hospital. He was also an artist; he painted portraits in oil and also worked in charcoals. He would earn extra money around town by painting advertisements for various companies. He was also a functioning alcoholic, which tended to make life a little interesting to say the least. He seemed to be in a lot of mental or spiritual pain most of the time. I used to look in his eyes and see a lot of pain and agony he seemed to put himself through; he never seemed to be at peace with himself or his life. Him being an artist at heart, I believe he was very stifled as far as what he really wanted to be and do in life. He also wrote poetry a lot. His life reminded me of a poem I read by Langston Hughes "Whatever Happens to a Dream Deferred?" This was my impression of my father. My parents had eight children, six girls and two boys. I know my father loved his family, but I'm sure he would have loved to just be who he was at heart, an artist. Anyway, we did the best we could and all managed to grow up and have families of our own. All of us but my sister Leigh.

As I said before, she was a very beautiful black female. My impression of her was that of a very strong person when she was a teenager. I was a few years younger than her; she was the third born in my family. My mother said that she was a very beautiful baby and she certainly was a beautiful young girl.

The reason why I thought she was strong was because of the way she was towards me. I was so much younger than she was, and as some older sisters can be towards younger ones, she seemed to get the most pleasure out of all the teasing that was directed towards me. She was the main one that would say hurtful things to me that cut very deeply. I guess that was why I always thought that she was so strong. But, she wasn't. I remember her dating while in junior high school.

There were lots of boys that liked her, three in particular, Lawrence Barnes, Paul Brown, and Frankie Warren, all very handsome young boys that would come by our house to see her. I wondered which one she would choose. Paul seemed very nice and Lawrence (Larry) was a light-skinned muscular boy who was an athlete. Frankie, a handsome darker-skinned muscular boy, was also an athlete; he was the star of the show as far as junior high sports was concerned. One day, I noticed that Paul and Larry stopped coming around anymore, but Frankie was always at the house. They fell in love and became an exclusive couple. They were very much in love, and were always together gazing into each other's eyes. But after a while I noticed that he acted as if he owned her. He turned out to be very controlling of her and very jealous; he never liked her wearing certain clothes. I remember him getting upset over her prom dress because he thought that the neckline was too low. It was just a regular A-line dress with a regular neckline that didn't expose anything .He made the statement that he did not want anybody looking at her neck! (Beware.) Anyway, they remained together despite his ways. She told me one day that the reason Paul and Larry stopped coming around was because Frankie threatened them. He was a really big and forceful-looking person and his presence could be pretty fearsome at times.

Leigh looked like a little bird beside him; she was so small and quiet when they were together. She took on a meek and mild appearance with him, so overshadowed, as if she was a lost puppy. Their eleventh-grade year turned everybody's life around, our family and his. I used to see them in very compromising positions; I don't think they knew that I would, on occasion, catch them making out. I remember one night, I was lying in bed and she decided that she would start in on me with the taunting about how ugly and dumb I was and I just couldn't take it any longer. "If you don't leave me alone, I'm going to tell Mamma what you and Frankie have been doing." She shut up right away and left me alone from then on.

One night, she got very sick and my parents took her to the hospital. They came back and Leigh was crying, but nobody told the rest of us what was up. Then, from time to time, I would hear my mother questioning her. The questions would be relentless; it seemed as if they went on forever. "What are you going to do? What is he going to do?" It seemed as if this went on night after night, I knew something was up, but what could it be? Then, there were the meetings between my parents and Frankie's parents. The arguments, the tears, I couldn't figure it out. I remember a white lady coming over to the house quite often to talk to Leigh. I couldn't figure out who she was or what she was doing at our house.

Then, one day, Leigh went away to a school in another part of the state. By then, I knew that she was pregnant, which was something that did not happen to girls every day back in the early '60s. Frankie's mother was a social worker and had arranged for Leigh to go away to a home for unwed mothers. That was why that white lady kept coming around; she was a social worker. I know this because I had one also when I was pregnant with Camille. She would come around to talk to me about my condition and how to take care of myself and what to do after my baby was born.

It was decided that Leigh would finish her eleventh-grade year at this home for unwed mothers, have the baby and then come back home as if nothing had happened.

I remember that July day when Frankie came running down to our house very excited and happy. My sister had given birth to a little girl; he was just smiling and shaking his head as if he could not believe that he was a daddy. He was truly happy; I could see that all over his face. He had been hanging around our house all the time that Leigh was gone, especially when school was out. He had a convertible; I believe it was red or blue. He came around the house one day and tried to get me to go for a ride with him; he said that he would pay me if I went with him. I knew that he had to be up to no good. I was just around twelve or thirteen years old, but every part of me said not to go. Why would he want me to go for a ride with him?

"No, I don't want to," I said.

"Why not? Sandra (my sister born after Leigh and before me) went with me one time." I knew he was lying. I did not like him very much and he seemed sneaky to me. Sandra told me that she saw him looking through our bedroom window one night while we were getting ready for bed. I knew he was up to no good.

When Leigh came back home, she went back to school to finish her twelfth grade. Her daughter, Francesca (we later called her Frankie), was placed in a home in the same town that we lived in. I really didn't know the circumstances behind her finally coming to live with us. I just know that all of a sudden, months later after she was born that we had a little baby girl living with us. She lived with us until her parents got married not long after they graduated from high school. While Frankie lived with us, I remember my mother questioning Leigh; it seemed, day after day, night after night "How are you going to take care of Frankie? Is he going to pay for milk for her, does he have a job? What about your education, are you going to finish school?" I was so young; I wasn't quite sure why Leigh was being put under the gun so hard.

Frankie got a job at the local 5 and 10 cents store and would buy milk and supplies for little Frankie whenever he could. I can remember my mom coming home from work some days and going straight to the refrigerator and shaking the milk carton to see if there was any milk inside. Years later, Leigh told me that she would put water in the carton to make it seem like there was milk inside. Those would be the days that Frankie would not have come by with milk for the baby. As I said, they got married soon after they graduated from high school. Frankie got an athletic scholarship to a big university in Ohio; he became their top football player.

They remained in Ohio until he graduated from college. They were very poor but they made it, they appeared to be very much in love. My sister gave birth to a little boy, Frank Jr. (of course). There seemed to be a pattern forming with both children being named after him. I guess he had always been "the star of the show" being an athletic hero all of his life. His parents' house was full of awards, plaques, trophies, and newspaper articles all about him. No wonder, he felt he was "all that" and I guess Leigh thought that he as also; she really loved him.

After college, he was drafted to the New England Patriots football team. Everyone was so excited and happy! That's when things started to go bad. While at the Patriots training camp, he broke his neck during football practice. Everyone was so upset, especially Leigh. I felt so sorry for her; she was devastated. He was rushed to the hospital and put in traction. Leigh came home and moved in with her in-laws with the two children. Everybody in town was sending up prayers for him and the whole family. Leigh and her in-laws would travel to Ohio to visit him while he was recovering. She would come back home from those visits devastated. "He has amnesia. He doesn't even know me or his parents, not even his children!" Leigh said to us with tears streaming down her face. No one knew what would become of Frankie; we all just prayed real hard.

Then, one Friday night, about one month after the accident, I was doing my favorite thing, talking on the phone to one of my friends, I can't remember who it was. All of a sudden, the front door swung open, and in jumped Frankie, dancing and just smiling and there was Leigh, behind him. She looked like a little girl, so small and petite; she had a smile on her face the size of Texas. People would mistake her for Frankie's daughter sometimes when they would go out, he was so big and she, so small.

Nobody could believe what we saw, but there he was in the flesh, as big and as bad as ever, just dancing and smiling. Everyone ran up to him and just hugged him. We were all thankful to God that he was back with us. I could see how much Leigh loved her man; she just could not stop looking at him. So much in love and so happy and blessed!

He could no longer play football; it would be detrimental to his health if he even thought about playing again. He landed a job with the FBI and was stationed out of Washington, D.C., during the week and he came home on the weekends. They had a lovely house one block over from both sets of parents' houses on a quiet street. Everything seemed to be going fine.

By this time, I had graduated from high school and was working downtown at the local five and dime store I was still dating David, but he seemed to be pulling away from me. He had received a scholarship from college in a little town in Alabama right after graduation and left town bound for glory. It turned out that his athletic scholarship and college was not what he thought it would be. He soon returned back home along with some of the other black athletes that went on to make their mark on the world . By the end of the summer the few black athletes that seemed to have it all in high school had returned home. What was it that made them come back so soon? None of them seemed to have a chance at success outside of our small town; they all came back home. David was determined that he was not going to be caught up with that small-town mentality; he was going places too and was going to be somebody. He decided to move to New York to live with one of his aunts, but he returned home soon after he left. He did all of this in just a few months' time. "What are you going to do now, David?" I asked him one hot summers' night; we were sitting on my front porch.

"I'm not too sure, but trust me; I will get out of this town, just wait and see." I was hoping he would say something about me going with him, but that never entered our conversation.

I started spending more time with Leigh; she was afraid to stay by herself at night. So she asked me to come and stay with her on a few nights during the week while Frankie was away at work in D.C. We got pretty close and became friends; it probably was because I had gotten older and we could relate more to one another. The only thing that I didn't like was that she would not let David come over to see me at her house. That made me angry; I figured that Frankie told her not to let him come over.

Frankie was very puzzling at times; I believe that at this point, Leigh was suspecting that he wasn't everything that she thought or that he was changing. She showed me a picture of me that came up missing from our family album. I was around fifteen at the time that the picture had been taken. I was sitting on the sofa, talking on the phone, I had my legs crossed and you could see up my dress a little and it showed a lot of my legs. She had found it in his wallet. I don't think she ever asked him about the picture. She never suspected that anything was going on between the two of us, it was like she knew that he had taken that picture for whatever reason, I don't know. I continued to stay with her, but on the weekends, when he would come home I would leave; it seemed as if the whole attitude of the household would change when he came home. He kept his job for a short time and then I guess he wanted to be close to his family. So he came back home to live and got a job at the same high school we all graduated from. He became the football coach there and taught a class in history.

I'm sure he was more than disappointed that his life did not turn out the way he had planned it; being a pro football player was far more glamorous than being a high school football coach. I believe this, along with what my sister would confide to me, affected his mind. She thought that maybe something happened to him while he was in traction; after all, he had two holes drilled into his skull. I don't know if this contributed to his change, but he did change. I guess life can do you in if you let it.

They moved into a larger house and settled down to everyday living. He would go out to work every morning and leave her at home with the kids. There she would be, all day long, just she and the two children.

She became a prisoner in her own home. He didn't want her to drive, work, go back to school, nothing. The only place she would go was to visit us at our house and maybe to his parents' house.

One day, while she was visiting us at our mom and dad's, it was a Saturday afternoon. We were all on the front porch waiting for him to pick Leigh and the kids up and take them back to their prison. When we heard all these sirens, a few moments later, some friends of the family came by to tell us that Frankie had been in a car accident just a block up the street from the house. Leigh was very upset when she got into their car to go to the hospital; her head was lowered and she was crying. He was in traction again, this time in the local hospital. He had to be cut out of the car, a four-stop intersection. We never really got the story on that accident because the events of that Saturday and the days that followed would change my family's life forever.

In the days that followed, Leigh spent a lot of time with us. She had my mom down to spend the night with her and the kids; she and the kids spent the night with Frankie's grandmother, something that never happened; I did not know that they were so close. Leigh called me one night that week and asked me if I had heard anything about Frankie running around on her, being with other women. I did not go out that much because of my work and coming home taking care of my daughter. "I haven't heard anything, but if I do, I will let you know" is what I told her.

My day off was Thursday afternoons from the dental office I worked at. That Thursday I spent the afternoon with Leigh. We had a nice time talking and eating. She was a little tired from running over to the hospital to see about Frankie; the hospital was only a block away from their house. But she had been going there every night to see him. She began talking to me about leaving him. "I want to leave him, but I am afraid that I would never get rid of him, he would follow me to the ends of the earth," she told me. We went upstairs to their bedroom. She opened her closet, which was full of clothes, brand-new clothes with the tags still on them. "Where do I go to wear these clothes? I didn't even get a chance to pick these clothes out! He bought all these clothes for me, but he never takes me anywhere; I only get to go to Mom's on the weekend. When we go out together, I can't even look at another man or if one looks at me, he will go off and ask me if I want a divorce!" she said angrily. I could see that she was miserable, a prisoner.

She had been troubled with stomach problems for the last year, but the doctor could not find anything wrong with her. Could it have been the stress of living with her husband that caused her health problem? I remember her telling me that, one night, they were getting ready to go to bed and he fixed her a Coke to drink. She said after she drank it, she started feeling funny and started seeing things on the wall, animals and strange things. "I had an incredible urge to jump out of the window, because I didn't like the way I was feeling," she told me.

He spiked her drink! I remember thinking. How could he do that? Only the lord knows what all she went through.

That Thursday that I spent with her was the last time I was to see her alive. I spent the entire afternoon with her and the children. My brother James stopped by while I was there to see her. That was something he never did; I remember thinking how strange that was. After I left (I had my baby daughter with me), I went home, pushing her in the stroller while my younger sister Lizzie arrived at Leigh's house to watch the kids while she went to the hospital to see Frankie. I can't remember when Lizzie came home; I just remember that our phone was not working that afternoon for some reason. I remember that because I called home before I left Leigh's house and I couldn't get through.

The next day, everything as usual, everybody got up to start his or her daily duties, work, school, whatever the day called for. I went to work that morning and worked until my lunch hour. I walked home for lunch and to feed Camille; I would do this every day. When I got there, my oldest sister was home; she stayed home because she was slightly retarded and could not work. "Mom is at the hospital. Something happened to Leigh," she said. I called the hospital and found Momma; she didn't sound too upset.

"Leigh has been shot," she said. I couldn't put any of that together in my mind.

Who would shoot her? I thought to myself.

Was it the guy that lived in the garage apartment behind their house? What in the world is going on? I thought. "I'll be right out there," I told her. I don't remember how I got to the hospital. I just remember being there and waiting with my parents. Frankie was not in the hospital anymore; for some reason, he was down in the emergency room with a badly cut hand. He had left the hospital the night before; he had taken himself out of traction and walked home. My mom asked me to go down to the emergency room to see if he was all right. I didn't want to, but I did. He was down there, soaking his hand in a basin; he looked terrible. I asked him if he was all right. He just shook his head yes. I went back up to the waiting room and just—waited with everyone else. She was in surgery.

I ask what had happened to her, why and how was she shot? Self-inflicted—self-inflicted? No way, that couldn't be right. The doctors said that she was shot in the shoulder. In the shoulder—I figured that was not too bad, she would recover. But why would she do that? Was she trying to warn Frankie about something, trying to send him a message? I couldn't understand the whole situation. The surgery was taking a very long time for just a shoulder wound. Finally, after what seemed like forever, the surgery was over and the doctors came out to talk to my parents. I don't know where Frankie or his parents were, it only seemed like my parents and I were there the whole time. The doctors told them that the bullet that entered her body through the shoulder was the type that exploded once it got inside of her. Her injuries were very extensive. The bullet broke a few ribs and this caused one of the ribs to puncture her lungs. She was bleeding internally.

Everything got really dreamlike from that point. Momma told me to go home to watch after Camille, who was just five months old at that time. Daddy drove me home; the ride home was silent, both with our own thoughts I suppose. My sisters Lizzie and Janie, my brothers Jeremy and James and my daughter were all at home when I got back. I remember going up to my bedroom and looking out of the window not knowing what to feel. If I prayed, I don't remember. Just nothing, I could not feel anything, didn't know what or how I was supposed to feel. I went downstairs and my sister Lizzie was feeding Camille, I remember that.

Then, the phone rang. I didn't want to answer; it was my mother. "Leigh is gone, she passed," is what she said. "Have James go tell the Warrens." She hung up. She sounded so in control. How could she sound so in control when her daughter had just died? Leigh, dead at age twenty-four.

I told my brother what my mother said to tell him. He ran out of the house to go up the street to tell the Warrens what had happened. Everyone was crying—disbelief. All of a sudden, it seemed like everybody started calling at the same time to find out about Leigh. I remember answering the phone one call after another and having to tell people over and over that she had died. I was just nineteen and in such a daze, everything was upside down. Both of my sisters, Anna who lived in Michigan, and Sandra, living in New Hampshire, called and I had to tell them that our sister was dead. I will never forget the wailing that I heard on the other side of the phone. So very mournful, so full of anguish, just terrible, terrible, and terrible is the only way to explain the sound. I will never forget those mournful outpourings I heard that night; I will always carry those sounds with me.

Everything was so confusing; the days to follow seemed to run together. I remember a tremendous outpouring of sympathy for Frankie. Here he was, a young widower with two small children, walking with a cane from his latest accident. The sight of them painted a very sad picture. I remember seeing them, all three, walking down the street a few days after Leigh's death. I was sitting on the front porch and he was walking down the street leaning on his cane, one child on either side of him. His head was lowered; they all looked so lost. Everybody was lost, not knowing how to cope with this sudden tragedy; one day, everything is just fine and the next day, everything is so wrong.

All of the family came in, Anna and Sandra, my two sisters, were the only ones of us that lived out of town at that time. The rest of us, Janie, myself, James, Lizzie and Jeremy, all lived at home. My cousins, aunts, uncles, old family friends from years ago came in. My beloved grandmother, my father's mother came in from our hometown in southern West Virginia. She was so disoriented when she entered the house, she could not distinguish one of us from the other. She would look me in the eyes so deeply, and she asked me "Which one are you?" she was so far gone with grief. Death is not a very nice part of life is it? The day of her funeral, all I can remember is coming downstairs and, halfway down the staircase, looking over at a sea of people, my people, my family and all of our friends. Gathered together to say goodbye to our Leigh and to support one another in love and hope for the future. She was gone from us forever, but she will always be in our hearts. Her children were ages six and two years old.

So many questions surrounding this incident started to surface. Why was there not a note if she committed suicide? What happened between the time Lizzie left Leigh's house and the next morning? Why did Frankie remove himself from traction and walk home that night? Where did that gun come from? Lizzie says that Leigh had started receiving phone calls one after the other after she arrived at her house. They appeared to be crank calls from some girl is what Lizzie could gather. Leigh left to go to the hospital; she was a little upset when she left and also when she came back. It seems that she had walked in her husband's hospital room and found a woman there, and that was not the first time she found her there. It was the same woman that was calling her that night. Elaine Hudson, she went to high school with Leigh and Frankie. Elaine was a very cute girl; I remember seeing her at different high school events I would attend with Leigh and Sandra from time to time. Also, the town was so small, everybody knew everybody anyway.

Later that night after Leigh came back home according to Frankie, she called him at the hospital and said that she had taken a bottle of pills. He called his mother and begged her to bring him some clothes out to the hospital because he did not have any since they had to cut him out of the car and, I suppose his clothes. Whether or not she brought him his clothes is unclear. Whichever case, he ended up at home. He said he called Leigh's doctor and he told him to walk her all night and that is what he said he did. In the morning, he says that he went back to the hospital to check out because they called him and told him to either come and get back into traction or check out so he went to check out. Apparently, while he was at the hospital, his wife got his gun, which belonged to the FBI; he was supposed to return it when he left that position, but, apparently, he did not. She got the gun and shot herself in the shoulder.

Little Frankie says she heard her mommy calling her and that when she went up to see what she wanted her mommy was lying on the bedroom floor moaning. She was a very bright little girl to be so young. She knew her mommy was sick so she ran next door and told the neighbors that something was wrong with her mommy and they called the ambulance. Somehow, my brother James received a call from Little Frankie and bolted out of our house and ran to Leigh's house. He found her in a pool of blood, lying beside her bed. These are the events as far as we could put everything together. When the police arrived, they could not find the gun at all.

I'm sure, since they are professionals that the first place they would have looked would have been beside her body. However, Frankie found the gun under the bed that she was lying beside. This was what was told to my family by one of the investigating officers that just happened to be a good friend of my sister Anna. There was no investigation of her death; it was ruled as a suicide and left at that. So, I guess that it was and we will never know for sure what really happened to her, just that she is gone.

Chapter 3

The song says "Everything must change, nothing stays the same." So it was with us after she left. My brother did not cope with finding our sister in the shape she was in; he didn't cope well at all. He never talks about that day. I just know that he suffered a lot and for a long time after that eventful period. He was younger than I was, about seventeen years old.

Life still goes on and about a week after the funeral, I went back to work and tried to put things back together again. I worked long hours at the dental office. Dr. William Kennedy was my boss and he was a very good man; however, he was quite stingy as far as my pay went. I worked from 7:30 a.m. until 6:00 p.m. Monday through Saturday, getting only Thursday afternoons off.

It being a dental office, sometimes as in any medical office, your appointments would run over and sometimes I would not get home until 7:00 in the evenings. I was tired a lot. Dr. Kennedy was getting up in age by the time I came to work for him. Like most senior citizens, he liked to talk a lot about his life and times. He liked to tell everyone about everything that happened to him over and over again. Of course, I knew a lot of his stories by heart. He was quite a character.

I became pregnant the first month that I worked for him; I was a very small young girl, size three, so it took a long time for anyone to tell that I was going to have a baby. I did spend a lot of time in the bathroom throwing up those first four months. I was very sick, but I continued to work, standing on my feet all day long assisting the doctor with the patients. I would walk to work every morning, walk home for lunch at noon, and walk back to work for the afternoon and walk home from work at the end of the day. I had no social life, but that was all right. All I could do was think about my little baby that I was carrying around inside of me.

David was gone away in the Navy; he left in January of that year. I became pregnant in December, one month before David left for basic training. I started getting sick and throwing up morning, noon, and night. I suspected that I was pregnant and told him what I suspected when he called to say goodbye to me. "Latisha does not want to have any brothers or sisters" was his comment to me after I told him my suspicions (Latisha was his first child's name, and she was born right before he went into the twelfth grade). He told me that he would get in touch with me when he could, and that he would send me his address so that I could write to him and tell him for sure. Then he left, but I knew that he would not desert me and he didn't.

This would be the test, I thought. He could just disappear from my life forever if he wanted to. But, I knew him; I was positive that he loved me and would not leave me.

I decided not to be like one of those girls that tried to hide their secret from everybody. I didn't have time for all of that. I just decided to tell my mother why I was taking a full day off . She woke me up that morning and asked me why I was not going to work. "I have a doctor's appointment," I told her. Well, of course, her being a woman and not a dumb woman put two plus two together and got baby.

"So, here you are, pregnant and he has left you!" she yelled.

I was still lying in the bed. I looked her in the eyes and said, "He hasn't left me, Mamma."

"Yes he has, he's gotten what he wanted out of you, now you're pregnant and he has ran away to the Navy. You'll never see him again!" she continued to yell.

"I will hear from him again." He promised me that he would write and I knew he would, I felt he would deep down inside. I did not waver from my belief because I knew him so well.

I went to the doctor and, of course, he told me what I already knew. I walked home from his office not feeling any different physically. I guess I was expecting to feel different somehow. But, I felt the same as I did before the doctor confirmed my condition. When I went in the house, Daddy was in the kitchen preparing his lunch. He asked me why I was home, I told him, and all he said was "Well, my insurance can't pay for anything," that was it from him. I suspect my mother had already told him what was up.

Not much was said about my condition, I just continued to work and grow big. I wasn't ashamed of my pregnancy at all. As a matter of fact, I was proud to be pregnant, especially by David Houser. I tried to poke my belly out way before it started poking out on its own. I especially tried to poke it out whenever I would see Tonya on the street or any of her girls.

As all small towns go, news travels fast and before you know it, everybody knows about everybody's business. One evening, while I was still at work, the phone rang. I picked it up. "Dr. Kennedy's office," I said. It was Tonya, I recognized her voice immediately.

"I heard some news about you and I want to know if it is true. I heard that you were pregnant and that it was David's baby. Is this true?"

I was so happy she found out, I was so cool and collected, it surprised me. "Yes, it's true, but, listen, I can't talk here at work. Why don't you call me at home, I'll be there about 6:30 this evening." It sounded as if she had started crying.

"Okay, I'll call you later," was all she could say. I hung up and couldn't wait until I got home to tell her everything. After all, she was my archenemy. All those times in high school that she and her friends used to antagonize me; I was ready to tell it all to her after all the grief she gave me in the past.

As luck would have it, we ended up in the same gym class; she was in the tenth grade and I was in the twelfth. Her best friend was in that class also. Every other day during gym, I guess they rehearsed a script before they came to class. "Tonya, did you see David last night?" her friend would ask.

"Oh, yes, we had a wonderful time, just he, and I, and our daughter," she would reply. They would always make sure I was somewhere close by so I could hear them. It turned into a game; I started doing the same thing with my friends. We'd rehearse our script, and then we'd go in for the kill.

One morning at school, I spotted her going into the bathroom; this was my perfect chance. David had been over to my house the night before and I had a big hickey on my neck. I had tried to cover it with a pair of very large earrings, the kind that was in style back then, especially if you happen to be sporting a very large "Angela Davis" Afro like I was. In we went, ready to strike! My friend: "I don't know why you are trying to hide that big passion mark on your neck with those big earrings, I can still see it. Did David do that last night?"

"Ohhhh God, can you see it? I hope my mom didn't notice it this morning!" I exclaimed.

We pretended that we did not see Tonya standing there, but of course we knew all along that she was there. She almost burst into tears and ran out of the bathroom. This puzzled me; she always seemed so street worthy and tough. There were a few times that I thought we would come to blows, one time in particular. Someone started a rumor that I was talking about her baby, and one day, after school, she and her best friend confronted me.

"I heard you have been talking about my baby!" she exclaimed.

"Why would I talk about your baby, I don't even know her!" was my reply. I was nervous, because I was never one to fight; however, I'm sure I would have defended myself quite well if it came down to blows.

"Well, if you ever do, I'm going to kick your ass," she said.

"I don't think David would like that too well, do you?" was my reply. After I said that, she just backed off and they went down the hall. My heart was beating so fast I thought it was going to jump right out of my chest. Just as fast as it was beating now that I was home and the phone was ringing, I knew it was her.

"Hello," I said. It was Tonya. "What do you want to know?" I asked her.

"Is David really the father of your baby?"

"Yes he is," I said.

"How could that be? He told me that you two had broken up a long time ago and that even when you were together that you only did it a couple of times." She sounded very upset.

"He was always at my house, Tonya, at least every other night." I knew he spent the other nights with her. "We've been together lots of times."

"How many?" She sounded as if she was crying by this time.

"Oh, hundreds of times," I said. "He's the only one I have been with and if he told you we've only been together a few times, then he is lying."

She just hung up. I knew she was upset. I started realizing something; she loves him too, just as much as I loved him, and he had been lying to her. He never lied to me; I knew where he was when he was not with me, because he told me. I always let him talk when we were together. He would pour his heart out to me about all of his feelings, about Tonya, and their daughter, how he felt about them and how he felt about me. I always knew what was up with all of us. She didn't, because she would never want to hear about him and me. He would try to tell her about how he felt about me and how he felt about her, but she would always say, "I don't want to hear about that bitch!" This is why she was so hurt and surprised when she heard that I was pregnant with his child. I'm sure this broke her heart. In the end, both of us had broken hearts, I suppose. I gave birth to Camille on September 15, 1972. After I had her, I went back to work and got my figure back—that's easy to do when you are young.

Chapter 4

After the death of my sister, I didn't want to do anything, just hang around the house. One night, my girlfriend Teresa came by with some more of our girlfriends and convinced me to go to the neighborhood recreation center for a dance. I didn't want to go, but I went since I knew they were trying to make me feel better. I had a pretty good time; I walked in and just stood around at first. Then I noticed a guy staring at me very intently. "Hey, that's that girl that works for Dr. Kennedy!" I heard him shout over the music. I recognized him from my job. He came up to the office one day to talk to Dr. Kennedy about something. I remember hearing the waiting room door opening, I looked out to see who had entered the area and all I saw was a young man, tall, light skinned and very thin, with a hard hat sitting on top of his Afro and some dirt right on the tip of his nose. He was not what I was expecting to see when I peered out of that window. I started cracking up laughing; the sight was so funny. The girl that was working with me asked me what was so funny. I was laughing so hard, I could not even talk, I just pointed up at the window, and she looked out and started laughing herself.

"You go out and see what he wants," I said.

"No, you go see," she said.

"I can't, I just can't, did you see that dirt on the end of his nose?" I asked her. She refused to go out there to receive him, so, I got myself together and opened the door then poked my head out into the waiting room. "May I help you?" was all I could get out without bursting into another fit of laughter.

"I would like to see Dr. Kennedy if it is possible," he said.

"May I have your name please?"

"Yes, Darnell Moneymaker," he replied. I had heard that name before. He had been calling the office for a week looking for Dr. Kennedy. But he was out of town attending a dental conference.

When he left his name the first time he called, all I could think was *Moneymaker, what kind of name is Moneymaker?* Little did I know that in a few years, that would be my name also.

I really was not in the mood for dancing that night. I felt funny being there; after all that had happened I didn't feel too much like having fun. I would dance with different guys every now and then; I just moved around the floor a lot that night trying to get into the spirit of the night. I noticed that every place I moved to, this dude was staring at me. It didn't matter which part of the floor I was standing, I would look up and see him either standing against the wall staring at me or sitting in a chair. I thought, that's the guy that was at the office a few weeks ago! I started feeling pretty special and started getting interested in him. After a while, he came over to me and asked for a dance. He could dance really good. We did all the latest steps, especially the bump and the robot, which was very big then.

It was 1973 and Afros and bell-bottoms, Dashikis, and halter-tops were the rage in fashion and let's not forget those platform shoes! We danced on every song that was played. Back then, we had live bands and the music was so good, and the thump of the bass made you feel that you could dance forever. We danced to the fast songs and the slow songs; in between, we would talk. I was very impressed that he was a college man and I could tell by his accent that he was not from West Virginia. Most of the guys that I grew up with did not go to college, and they felt threatened by any of the young black male college students that attended the local university. What is it about some black people that make us feel threatened or inadequate when we see someone else in our race trying to do well for themselves? Instead of being happy for one more black person trying to make it in this world, we become mad or jealous. The university sat on one side of the viaduct at Martin Luther King, and the black community sat on the other side. This viaduct represented a line or barrier drawn between the "local" blacks and the black "college" students that thought they were better than the local people. Of course, that was not true, but I found that the local guys always felt this way for some reason; I know that there was always a fight when the college students tried to do something, like have a dance or function at the community center. There were all kinds of comments being made like "Why don't ya'll stay on the other side of the viaduct where ya'll belong" or " Y'all think y'all better than us just because ya'll in college." I know that one reason why there was a rift between the two sides was because a lot of the local girls would go hang out on campus. I know this because I would hear a lot of girls talking about their experiences on campus, who did it with who, who they thought was fine. Some of these girls were much younger than me, and they'd be over there all the time.

Back to the dance… As we danced all night, I noticed that people were staring at us as they would walk by or dance by. I kept wondering why everybody was looking at us. I figured it was because I was dancing with "one of those college guys." By the time the dance was over, I felt very intrigued by this guy. I was a little overwhelmed. "A dude from college, interested in me?" This was not happening I thought.

"Can I walk you home?" he asked.

"Yes, I don't live too far from here. I came with my girlfriends, but I'm sure they will understand." As we walked the two blocks to my house, I noticed people driving by staring—what's the deal? Anyway, halfway down the block, he stopped me and took me in his arms and kissed me very deeply. Oh boy, did that feel good! I hadn't been kissed in a long time, months! Not since David and I split up for good that December. It was around April or May when I met Darnell.

"I hope you did not get offended by me kissing you," he said, "but I couldn't help myself."

"No, that's okay, I didn't mind," I said. I thought, *What a gentleman! I think this might go somewhere.* I wanted him to kiss me

33

again. I was still very young and naïve even though I had a baby, that fact doesn't make you experienced in life. I was just eighteen years old. When he kissed me, it felt good all over my body; that feeling you get down in the pit of your stomach and it spreads to every part of your being, it was so strong. Looking back on it, I was just horny! I still didn't know too much about my body. All I know is that by the time we finished making out and talking on my front porch, I had made up my mind to go to bed with him. While we were on the porch talking, my brother James came up. He was at the dance also, and he spoke to Darnell by name. Well, my brother knew him, I thought. He must be pretty well known with everyone looking at us tonight and my little brother knowing him. "I want to see you tomorrow. Will you come to my apartment?" he said after a particularly long kiss. My knees were getting week and I was very aroused.

"Yeah, where do you live?" I felt all grown up; I'm going over to his apartment! I was stepping over into another dimension; I'd never known anyone with his or her own apartment! A man, at that, and to think that I would be actually going over to see him at his apartment! I felt so grown up.

We talked for a long time, he told me he was from Tallahassee Florida, and that he had come to the university on a football scholarship. Darnell was a very handsome young man, very tall, thin and he had the biggest puppy dog eyes! He put me in the mind of Gregory Hines. Everywhere we've gone, people have asked him if he was kin to Gregory Hines. As far as I know, he's not but he does look a lot like him.

We talked about a lot of things, his school, my job; the usual get-acquainted conversation that everyone has. While listening to him talk, I decided that I would tell him about my baby; I loved Camille so much, and I would never put her aside for anyone. I decided that I would tell him that night, and if he rejected me because of that, then he was not worth my time. "I need to let you know that I have a little baby girl; she was born last September." I was waiting for some type of reaction from him, but I couldn't read what was going on in his mind. He just accepted this information very calmly. He said that he was fine about that and that it really didn't matter. I was amazed at this; he seemed so nice. I was sure he would run when I told him that I already had a child. But he didn't, he said he wanted to be with me. So that was that. *What a guy,* I thought to myself

He told me where he lived, near the university in a house that had been converted into a few apartments for college students. We finally said goodbye, he left and I floated into the house. All I could think about was the next day; I got up early the next morning, which was Sunday. I knew I couldn't stay home that morning, no way in our house, all of us would get up every Sunday and go to Sunday school and church. I had to usher that particular Sunday anyway. I was a little sleepy, but all I could think about was going to see Darnell later on that day. Around 3:00 was the time we set. Of course I would walk, because like I said, everybody walked in that town. In the spring and summer on Sunday afternoons after church, everybody would hit the streets in their Sunday best and just stroll from avenue to avenue, stopping and talking to people on their porches or whomever they would happen to run into.

I got to church and all of us girls were telling each other about our night during and after the dance. I thought that I had found me a treasure, someone that's not from this town and a college student at that, and he didn't mind about Camille! After church, I was walking home with a friend of mine that was attending college at that time. She asked me how well I knew Darnell; I told her that I had just met him last night. "Did you know that he was married?" I felt like I had been hit in the stomach with a ton of bricks.

"Uh no, no, I didn't know that." I was so shocked, that was all I could say.

"Did you know that he had a kid? "she asked.

"No, I didn't know he had a kid either. No wonder he was so calm when I told him about Camille!" I felt like a fool; here I thought I was revealing something that would make or break what could be a potential relationship, and this man has all kinds of secrets going on. *They are all the same,* I thought. *Well, I'm going to tell him off when I hear from him today. He is supposed to call me before I go over to see him. I don't understand one thing, if he is married and has a kid, where are they and why does he live alone?* I couldn't wait to talk to him. The strange thing was, I still wanted to be with him.

I was home for a few hours going over in my head, the night before, how it felt to be with him and the newness of all the events from the night before was still very exciting to me. When the phone rang, my heart started beating fast. It was him, I picked up the phone. "How are you today?" he asked.

"I'm fine, and how are you, Mr. Married Man?" I just let him know up front what I had found out about him.

"Wow, it didn't take you long to find that out. Yes, I am married but we are separated. My wife and son don't live here in town. I guess you don't want to be with me now, do you?" I thought about it and that little voice (at that time, the voice was very little) said that I should just leave him alone. But that other voice said that I was horny and that it would be just this once.

"No, I want to come to see you. I'll be there around 3:00." (Beware, girl.)

So, at 3:00 I showed up at his apartment, thinking I was so grown up. He was waiting for me in the downstairs hallway. There seemed to be two large apartments downstairs and two upstairs, or maybe four apartments on each level. He lived upstairs in a one-bedroom apartment. It was a nice little place with a living room/kitchenette and a small bathroom off from the living room.

The apartment smelled like incense, which was a normal smell for a lot of places seeming how that was the latest thing, burning incense. We sat down on his sofa and he started explaining his situation to me. He came up here from Florida to go to school, he met this girl and they started dating. He was on the rebound from his high school sweetheart back home, that he had planned to marry. I don't know if she knew this fact or not, but he said that he wanted to marry her. After their breakup, he started dating Evelyn, they got to fooling around and, well, you know what happened. She got pregnant and he just decided to marry her. He didn't love her, just decided that was the right thing to do. So that's what he did. Now, they did not live together as he was staying in that apartment with a frat brother of his (he is a "Q" dog) and his wife was living with her mother in a small coal mining town in southern West Virginia which just happened to be the same town that I was born in!

After he told me his story, I felt a little better; it wasn't like he was *"actively"* married. All I knew was that I wanted him to make love to me that day, that's all I wanted. Soon we got to fooling around and the next thing I knew, we were lying on the bed and both of us had our clothes off. I don't know what I was expecting, I guess I was expecting him to make love to me the same way that David did, him being the only other lover I had in my entire young life. He was a pretty good lover, however, it's just that I was surprised that he was different than David, his style was different. I was so naïve, what a thing to think that everyone would be the same!

Anyway, we spent the rest of the day just lying around, and talking, making love and getting to know each other. "I'd better go." I finally decided that I'd better get home to my baby. I'd been gone all day and I knew my mamma would be on me for staying gone so long. Darnell sweated a lot and my hair was not looking as good as it did before I left home earlier that day; I hoped Mamma would not pay any attention to one side of my hair being kinkier than the other. He put me in a cab and, as I rode away, I looked back and saw him just standing there watching the cab pull away from him. He looked very sad; I couldn't figure that out. I got home; I can't remember the lie I told Mamma as to why I came home in a cab, I just know that I went straight to the kitchen and straightened my hair with the hot comb.

He called me later that night, and we talked for a long time, we decided to see each other on my afternoon off. He called me every night and we would talk for hours, sometimes until the wee hours of the morning. My mom would start fussing at me about staying up all night on the phone, leaving her lights on in the living room all night. So, I started turning the lights out but still we would stay on the phone all night sometimes. It was during one of these all-nighters that he revealed to me that he not only had a son, but a daughter! Two kids, how could I compete with all of that?

"Why didn't you tell me that you had two children?"

"I knew how you felt when you found out about the one. I just waited before I told you about the second," he replied. By then, his wife and two children were in Florida with his parents. He did not know that she had packed the children up and arrived on his parents' doorstep until it happened. He was very upset to say the least. He thought she was still with her mother.

He told me that he loved me after we had been together only a few times. He looked me deep in the eyes with those big puppy dog eyes of his and told me that he had loved me from first sight. I wanted to tell him that I loved him back, but I just couldn't, because I didn't. Even knowing this fact, I still made it up in my mind that I was going to tell him that I loved him too. My plans were to tell him the next week. I guess, I thought that if he loved me, then I was just supposed to love him back.

We had fun together; he introduced me to a whole new world. The college world, his frat, his friends, everything was just so different than what I was used to. We would go out to dances sponsored by a fraternity or sorority. These young people seemed different than the people I grew up with. All of them were from other parts of the country and doing something with their lives. I was infatuated with that world. So, one night, after we had made love in his apartment, he looked at me very deeply, with so much love in his eyes, he would always look at me this way, it made me feel very uncomfortable because I could not return the look. When you are truly in love, you can look deeply into your lover's eyes and just stay there for a long as you want. I couldn't do that. He would tell me that he loved me all the time.

This night, I told him back. "I love you, Doc" (that was his nickname for me). He called me Dr. C because of my white uniform I had to wear on my job at the dental office. He shortened it to Doc; he had a nickname for everybody.

"I love you too" I said. That was not entirely untrue. I loved him, but I was not *in love with him*. There is a difference. He was so happy when I told him that I loved him too. Why did I say those words and not really mean them? Not the way he wanted me to mean them. Still naïve, so very naïve! We went along with our courtship as if he was free. Why not? Everybody knew we were a couple, everything seemed cool. Then, one day, his wife came back.

Without telling him, she showed up at his apartment door, with the two kids in tow. He had no place for them to stay. They couldn't stay with him; he had a roommate who was his frat brother, so he arranged for them to stay with some mutual friends of theirs until he could figure out what to do. He was so upset. "We can't see each other for a while," he said sadly to me over the phone. I was not too upset about us not seeing each other for a while. That should have told me something.

"Okay, we'll be able to see each other every so often. It won't be that bad," I said. It just did not bother me that much. We would sneak and see each other. By this time, he had an apartment of his own. His wife was looking for a job and he was working full-time and helping her out. Somehow, she had found out about me—small wonder in that town—and filed for a divorce on the grounds of adultery, and naming me as the adulteress! Boy, am I a grown-up now or what? Now, I'm an adulteress and it's down in black and white!

I didn't care; it just didn't phase me one way or the other. I did feel a little sinful; after all, you know that's one of the Ten Commandments and I was breaking that law. I tried to put that guilt behind me, ignore that. After they got a divorce, things would be all right. We just continued to see each other, sneaking around. That just wasn't my style; I hated that. I remember one night while walking from the movies, Darnell spotted one of his old bosses from the local newspaper he worked at—Edward Shaver, a very good sportswriter for the local paper. Darnell thought a lot of Mr. Shaver and apparently cared what he thought. "Quick, hide, there's Ed. I can't let him see us together!"

I got mad. "I'm not hiding from **nobody**, are you ashamed of me or what?" I asked.

He tried all night to make it up to me. We caught a cab and went back to his apartment. This apartment was really run down, and it was overrun with roaches; the other tenants were your average "poor white trash" and very nasty and dirty. We could not get rid of those suckers. I told him the only way to get rid of them was to move. So that's what he did. He found a nice apartment on the top floor of a three-story brick

39

house right across the street from the local football stadium that was shared by the university and the local high schools. It was so cool; we could look out of the window and see the game for free!

It was in this apartment that he got me to smoke my first joint! Oh, happy, happy, fun, fun. I had never felt anything so great! I had just started drinking regularly on the weekends. I couldn't stand to taste beer and when I drank wine, I had to mix some 7-Up or Sprite in with it and lots of ice. When I did drink beer, I had to put ice in it also. But, boy did I love that reefer! It made me feel so uninhibited, so free. I found that I enjoyed being high and being with Darnell so, after that night, every time we were together in his apartment, which was every weekend, we would get blasted and listen to music; he loved music and had a pretty good sound system by that time. We would listen to Earth Wind and Fire, The Commodores, The Brothers Johnson , Rufus, Average White Band, and on and on. Such great music and of course the almighty "Funkadelic," Parliament. We partied, just the two of us all the time. The lovemaking was so enhanced by the effects of the reefer, it was great; I felt like I could just do anything with him when I was that way.

I seemed to like being with him only if I was high. Had I found a way to stay with someone that was totally and completely in love with me, but someone with whom I could not return that complete love? The answer is yes, yes, a thousand times yes! I really thought that I had a problem with expressing my feelings at that point in our relationship. I was really starting to have a hard time being with him sexually; I just knew that something was wrong with me, that I was incapable of having those normal feelings that a female should have for a man. The only time I felt really free to enjoy sex was while I was high. So, I stayed high, we stayed high during our entire courtship which lasted two years.

"I want to marry you," he told me one day after making love. I don't remember saying "yes" to him. Maybe I did, I just know that we planned to get married as soon as his divorce was final. He decided to go in the Air Force after he graduated from college. He graduated with a degree in journalism; he was becoming a very good writer. He also became interested in photography. He shot a lot of pictures around town, black and whites. I believe he fell in love with photography.

Chapter 5

We got married on February 13, 1975, in a wedding ceremony in the local judge's chambers. My mom, dad and sister Sandra attended our wedding. Everybody wanted to know why we did not have a church wedding? We told them that it was because we did not want to spend a lot of money on the wedding, which was partly true. Especially on Darnell's part; he never liked to spend a lot of money, and he was paying child support by then. He would pay her in cash, not getting a receipt in return from her. I told him that he should get some proof that he was paying her or she might try to pull a fast one on him. He didn't listen to me, told me that he knew her better than I did.

This might have been true, but I knew the female mind, because I was a female. I knew that as soon as she got wind of our engagement, things would change. As soon as the engagement announcement appeared in the newspaper, Evelyn tried to sue him for more money. Tried to say that he was not paying her what he was ordered to. Hell hath no fury is all I could say to him. The only reason I put my announcement in the paper was because I wanted people to see that I had gone on with my life after David had married Tonya.

I remember the day that they got married, Darnell and I had been together for almost a year. One of David's friends came down to my house to talk to me; he was trying to get me to go to the wedding. "Why don't you come to the wedding?" he asked.

"Are you crazy? What in the world would I look like going showing up at Tonya's house to watch her and David get married?" I still loved him, I knew it deep down, it would always be there, but I never allowed it to come up. To come up from that private place I buried it in; it had to stay put.

Anyway, I put my picture in the paper for everyone to see that I was happy and going on with my life. That's just what I did too, went on with my life. David was married and he and Tonya and their daughter were living in Florida and I was back home planning my wedding, not that there was a lot to plan. My sister gave me a shower. She was so young, Lizzie; she really didn't know what to do in order to give me a shower, so I brought all the invitations and decorations and refreshments. All she did was attend, but that was all right. Darnell didn't want me to have a shower; I couldn't understand why he didn't want me to have a wedding shower. I kept questioning him. "What's up with you going against me having a shower? It would be a good idea for us to have one considering we are starting out without anything at all. The gifts we get would be a good economical way to help us get started," I explained.

"Well, I just don't want to be setting up there with all those women," he said.

"Who said you were invited? This is for women only, no males allowed."

"Oh, well, in that case, I guess it's all right. I thought I would have to be there." This struck me as being odd, that he thought he would have to attend the shower. But what if that was required, would it have been so bad to attend a function on behalf of the two of you coming together as man and wife? Apparently so. This was a warning sign I did not, could not see as a look into my life as his wife. Another sign was on a few occasions, I would find him in such a deep funk that nothing I did would pull him out of it. He would just sit there, silent and withdrawn deep down within himself. I just saw a glimpse of that while we were dating.

I remember, one night, while at his apartment, he just went wild. I don't know what brought it on, he seemed to be all right, a little quiet is what I thought. He was trying to put a record on the turntable and for some reason, it wouldn't go on just right. All of a sudden, he started throwing all of his precious, and I do mean precious records. (He gave me a lesson on how to handle them.) "Always pick them up from the outside, never touch the record itself, try not to get any dust or your fingerprints on the record itself," he would tell me as he gingerly picked the record up showing me how it was done. Well, he was taking his albums out of the covers and throwing them around the room, out of the third-floor window, just going berserk it was as if he was a different person... (Beware.) But , naïve Carol just sat there, amazed at what I was seeing and not knowing what to do. After he calmed down, I tried to talk to him, tried to get him to tell me what was wrong. I couldn't get any response out of him. I finally called a cab and went home, bewildered. I never found out what was up with him that night, but I never forgot it either. He had a lot of built-up rage inside of him, but I stayed with him and we got married.

The ceremony was quick. Judge Lawrence Russell married us in his chambers, and he was late. That could have been another sign, I don't know. Anyway, I felt better getting married in a judge's chambers instead of church because I felt like such a sinner, my conscience was getting the better of me. I felt that I had been wrong, going out with him while he was still married and then him getting a divorce to marry me. Plus, I had read in the Bible that if you married someone that had already been married, but is now divorced that you would still be committing adultery. Plus, the minister at our church during that time had tried to hit on me a couple of times and I had become very disillusioned by him and did not want him to conduct the wedding ceremony.

He was a very charismatic minister, arriving at our church when I was in the twelfth grade. His charisma attracted a lot of youth to join church and our youth choir grew immensely. He liked to "rap" with us, we would hang out at his house all the time. A great man and a very good preacher, he put all of us kids in the mind of Dr. M. L. King. He didn't like me hanging around David for some reason; he never would let him in to any of our dances or get-togethers that we would have from time to time. I couldn't figure that out. I guess he was just trying to protect me from what he thought was the wrong element.

He had a job a few doors down from the dental office I worked at. Both he and his wife had regular jobs besides being the pastor and first lady of the church. On occasion, he would give me a ride if he would see me walking home for lunch to feed Camille. On one day in particular, he picked me up. "On your way home for lunch, would you like a ride?" I got into the car, we just talked about everyday things, how was work, my little girl, things like that. Then he asked me if I was all right financially.

"Yes," I said.

He asked me if there was anything that I saw downtown in the stores that I wanted just let him know. At first, I didn't get what he was saying, and then it hit home exactly what he was up to. Was he trying to buy me or what? I couldn't believe this was happening!

"No," I told him, I didn't need anything, that I was fine. By that time, we had reached my house, he said that he would come around in about an hour to pick me up to take me back to work. I didn't want him to do that; what was I going to do? Sure enough, after lunch, he drove up to the house and beeped his horn. I went out and got into the car, trying to figure out how to tell him that I would rather he not transport me back and forth on my lunch hour. Well, the car had come to a stop on the corner, just a few buildings down from my job. All of a sudden, he reached over and felt my breast. "Feels good," he said. My heart started pumping, I squirmed away from him.

"I will get out right here," I said and opened the car door and got out. He never tried to give me rides after that. I could not believe my pastor tried to feel me up! Neither one of us said anything about what had happened in his car that day.

That's another reason why I decided that I didn't want to have a church wedding, because I didn't want to have too much to do with my pastor after that episode. After the ceremony, Darnell and I left on the bus for our honeymoon in Columbus, Ohio. I don't know why we chose Columbus, we just did. He didn't have a car and I guess renting one never came up between the two of us. He just decided that we would ride the bus. All the way up, he was all over me. I felt very uneasy about displaying such affection in public. This baldheaded white man kept looking back at us and smiling. I didn't want him to be all over me like that. I couldn't understand why most people that are newly married and in love are oblivious to others around them. But not me, I just wanted to enjoy the ride up without him kissing all over me and touching me.

When we got to the hotel, we smoked a joint, and I felt better. We had something to eat and then I called home to talk to Camille. My mom told me that the judge that had married us earlier that day had left after the ceremony and flew to Florida, had a heart attack and died. Was this an omen? We stayed in Columbus for a few days and then rode the bus back home. The next day, he was to leave for basic training in Texas. We took a taxi out to the airport and he got on the plane and was gone. I thought I was supposed to feel very sad and upset that my new husband was gone for six to eight weeks. I tried to summon up those feelings. I was just worried that the plane would crash; I wouldn't want anything to happen to him.

I guess I loved him as much as I could but I was not in love with him. I rode the cab back home and continued to work and take care of Camille. I started to get excited about moving to a new town, even though I did not know exactly where we would be living. But it was still very exciting. Darnell finally got to come home on leave after basic training, and before he was to attend tech school. He was going to tech school for writing since he scored very high on his aptitude test in this field. I was a little nervous about seeing him again after so many weeks being apart. I waited up for him downstairs in my parents' living room; we would be sleeping on the sleeper sofa while he was there on leave. I had the sofa all pulled out and ready for us. It had gotten really late, when finally the doorbell rang and I let him in. I thought I was supposed to run into his arms or something, it seemed as if we really didn't know exactly what to do. The moment was too awkward for newlyweds who had been married for a total of four days before they had to part.

Something was wrong, not right at all, I felt so uncomfortable. We went to bed and made love, but there were no real union; the union that should have been for two lovers after they had been apart for so long, then finally together once again. I don't know if he felt anything similar or if he felt any awkwardness about that night. He stayed for the weekend, we spent one night at a local motel, and then he left for technical school. This school was at Fort Benjamin Harris, in Pennsylvania. After he left, I just went back to work; I didn't go out much, just to church. I started getting excited and anxious about starting my new life as a married woman. I couldn't wait to have my own home with my own things to go in that home. I was excited about being on my own, a wife and a mother and all this in a state other than West Virginia. After a few weeks, I found out that we would be stationed at an Air Force base in Florida.

Chapter 6

The base was right on the Gulf of Mexico in Florida. There had been some talk from the Air Force of us going up north to a base in Maryland, which was much closer to home than Florida. But Florida sounded very interesting to me and would be a lot of fun. All I could think about was the beach. I had always wanted to see the ocean, and now here was my chance. Plus, I had always wanted to live down south; this was as south as you could get. I never prayed to live in the south, I just always wanted to. You know how, when you were young, you and your friends would be sitting around telling each other all your hopes and dreams for the future. I wanted to live down south, I didn't want just "any" plain old person as my mate, I wanted someone that was "unique"; that was the word that I would use when I describe my future mate. I never really prayed for these things, but God does know the desires of your heart. So, I did get to live down south and my man was "unique" to say the least

After a few more weeks at technical school, all plans had been made for the move to Florida. Camille was two years old by then, almost three. It was springtime and I was starting to say goodbye to my friends; as a result, I realized that this was the first time I would leave my home, my brothers and sisters and, of course, my parents. I started to feel sad and scared; I was turning another corner in my life and stepping into adulthood. I stayed busy trying not to think about leaving everything and everyone I knew. I tried not to think about taking Camille away from my parents and her aunts and uncles. I was taking her into the unknown with a man that was going to be her father. If I had known God back then as I do now, I would have done a lot of praying. Darnell thought there was no God; he felt strongly about this. He said he did not believe in organized religion, that the church was full of hypocrites. How many times have I heard that excuse used for why people refuse to go to church? Anyway, Darnell thought that the reason that he had hard times in life was because there really was no God. Because, if there were, his life would be a lot better than it was. I was so young and naïve that I didn't even argue with him about it or try to present the real truth to him about God, nor did I see his opinions about God as a threat to our relationship.

The time came for us to get ready to leave and start our new life in Florida. The day before we left, we rented a U-Haul van; this was all we would need to fit everything we owned inside. We had no furniture and never even thought about trying to save money to buy any once we got settled. Looking back, we were floundering from the start.

The van sounded as if it would not make it out of town, let's not even think about it making it all the way to Florida. We took it on a spin around town the day before we were to leave.

"This van don't sound too good, Darnell."

"It's all right, we'll be able to make it. We probably won't be able to find another one at this time anyway," he replied. So, we packed that van with all our belongings, including one of my mother's favorite kitchen knives that we used for what reason, I don't know, but it was her good butcher knife. This knife, we discovered, was left on the floor of the van, which meant we had to unpack everything we had just packed to get the knife.

So, that's what we did, we found the knife on the floor of the van, then we loaded the van once again. By this time, it was pretty late, and everyone was tired. So we went to bed. I could not sleep too well. Our bag lunch for the trip was packed, the van was full of gas, all we had to do was to get up, get dressed and go. We had planned to leave very early, around four o'clock in the morning, but, as usual Darnell just couldn't get himself together in order for us to leave on time. He had no sense of time whatsoever and we were always late for everything. Finally, it was time. My mom was in the kitchen; I didn't know how to say goodbye to anybody! First I hugged my sisters, my little brother—where was my daddy? Upstairs lying on the bed in his favorite position, stretched out, hands tucked behind his head, legs crossed at the ankles, and his feet rubbing together back and forth, back and forth against each other. I bent down and hugged him. "Bye, Daddy," I said.

He had tears in his eyes. "Bye-bye, girl."

I left out of that room really fast, went downstairs and hugged my mother again; I can't remember what was said to her or how I got out of that house and into the van. I just got Camille, and put her in her little chair that fit just right in between the bucket seats of the van.

"Let's go if we're going," I said to Darnell. I looked over on that porch for the last time, and my father had come downstairs by then; he and my mother standing there side by side waved goodbye. We drove off and, around the corner, I ran into my other brother James riding a bike; he had not come home the night before. I didn't even recognize him; his face was all swollen and distorted. "What happened to you?" I asked

"I was in a car accident last night. Me and my friends had a car wreck at the park," he said. His eyes were so swollen, looking back on his condition, he looked just like my father did one night when he had come home from being out drinking. Someone had beaten him up pretty badly and his face was all swollen and distorted, just like my brother's was now. I hugged him goodbye, and told him to please take care of himself. I knew he was in a lot of trouble; ever since Leigh's death, he was trying to escape the horror of finding her the way he did with drugs and running around with the wrong crowd. I don't know what happened to him the night before, but he looked really bad. It broke my heart to see him that way. He rode off in one direction on his bike and we rode off in the other. I started crying, Darnell didn't offer any support for my tears, nothing was said; he just drove.

Once we got on the highway, I made myself stop crying, told myself to not look back, to look forward and that's just what I did. We got almost through Kentucky, when all of a sudden, the van started acting up really bad, shaking and chugging then finally, stopping. Luckily, there was a gas station nearby and we were able to call U-Haul to have them send another van out to us. This took about an hour. When it came, it looked much newer and in better shape than the one we had originally.

Once more, we unloaded that van and reloaded our belongings onto the second one and after about another hour, were on the road again. We had a pretty nice trip after that, talking about our future and what living in Florida would be like. We got to Birmingham, Alabama, and it started raining pretty hard. Darnell was trying to hurry to beat the time we had lost in Kentucky, and he was supposed to report to base the next day around 12:00 noon. So time was not on our side. We were running behind schedule, which would become a way of life with him I was to find out. Driving through the rain pretty fast, going around a sharp curve, we hit a slick spot and spun around about three or four times. While spinning, I saw a huge tanker truck coming straight for us. I was so calm, I felt like this was the end, but I was so calm. As it turned out, the van spun into someone's front yard and the tanker went flying past us blowing his horn. "Are you all right, Doc? Is Camille all right?" He was frantic. Camille cried a little, but we were all fine. We drove right out of that front yard and got back on the street to continue our journey. No one came out of the house to see what was up; I suppose there was no one at home.

We drove on for a few miles, getting closer and closer to the Alabama–Florida border. He was pushing that van as hard as he could, trying his best to make things work out the way he had planned it. We would be losing the daylight soon, and I was getting pretty nervous about going any further in the dark. But he wanted to trudge on anyway, trying to make it to Florida in that one day. So, we drove on until we heard a big pop and the van started vibrating. We had blown a tire, the front passenger side. Darnell was livid, very angry and frustrated. He was determined to get that tire fixed and start back on the road to Florida. We drove around on the tire until all the air was gone and we were riding on the rim looking for a garage that would fix the tire. People keep beeping their horns at us to tell us that we were driving around on the rim. I guess they thought who in their right minds would do such a thing and know that they were doing it? We finally found a garage and called around trying to get someone to come out and service the van. But because he had ruined the rim, no one could get to us until the next day.

Darnell was so mad I didn't know how to take him; all I wanted to do was to go somewhere and lay my head down. Everyone was tired and dirty, I was on my period and I wanted to take a shower. When he calmed down enough to think straight, he decided to find a motel for us to stay the night. The first one had no vacancies, which made him even madder. I tried to calm him down, "Let's just find another place, Darnell, that's all we need to do." He was fussing about the town being racist and he knew that place had a room, they just didn't want us to stay there because we were black.

We found a motel after what seemed forever. It was like he could not function under a lot of pressure. I felt that he was my husband and he was to make all the decisions, but the more that things went wrong, the more he lost control. I was so glad to get into that room and bathe Camille and myself; we were all just plain tired. After everything settled down and we were all in bed, he kept apologizing over and over again. "I'm so sorry, Doc. I guess you want to go back home after all of this, I didn't mean for this to happen, for it to be like this," he said in a sad voice. I knew he was frustrated and tired and really wanted to make a good impression on me as my husband.

"It's all right, Darnell, we will get back on the road in the morning and get to the base on time. Let's just go to sleep." I looked over at Camille and she looked so sweet sleeping. *If only a child again* is what I was thinking.

The morning came and the sun was shining and I felt better, a little rested but not much. Darnell went to make arrangements to get somebody out to fix the tire and I decided that now was the best time to try and learn how to braid Camille's hair. My sister Lizzie was the braider in the family, and she would braid Camille's hair for me all the time. That girl could braid your hair so tight that your eyes would be slanted by the time she got through. Well now it was time for me to learn how, so I just took a braid apart one at a time and combed that section out, then re-braided it and it turned out just fine. By the time I finished, the van was all ready for us to start out again.

I started liking the way the countryside looked. Everything was getting flat and I was seeing sand and it was very warm and I just loved it. The clouds hung so low, that it seemed like you could just reach up and touch them. We were well into our trip when we came to a two-lane dirt road that was really winding. This is why we had all that trouble yesterday, I thought, God was trying to slow us down, even though Darnell had other plans. I don't know if we would have made it down that road late at night in the shape that Darnell was in. After seeing the condition of the road, he admitted that it was good we had that blowout when we did. I wanted to tell him that I felt that God was looking out for us, but decided not to in light of how he felt about that subject.

We made it to the Air Force base around 11:00 that morning. From what I could see of the area, everything was in bloom and just beautiful. The palm trees of that area were very short trees that bore figs; they were just beautiful. We arrived at the office he was assigned to, the base newspaper office where he would be a staff writer. We waited and waited in that office, just the three of us wondering what was taking so long with someone letting us know what we should do next. We had to have temporary housing until we found a place to stay. After a while, some military men came in to tell us in a very embarrassed tone that we had been re-routed to the base in Maryland. No one told us though. When he said that to us, I was about to blow. I would have refused to go anywhere else after the hell we had just come through to get there! But, they said that since there was an apparent screw-up on someone's part and we were there, then we would stay. The only problem was they did not have any temporary housing ready for us.

They put us up in a nice motel until the next day then we could move into temporary quarters for a couple of weeks. After we got all settled into the room, Camille and I went out to look around and to get a couple of sodas.

"Mommy, I'm ready to go home now" is what she said.

"Camille, you are home now, this is where we are going to live for a few years, okay?" I felt bad; she was so young and did not understand exactly what was going on.

The next day, we moved into a nice little place and started figuring out our next move. We went out to get some supplies, a little food and toiletries, things like that. The apartment was supposed to be equipped with all the essentials like pots, pans, dishes, etc. We just decided to have hot dogs the first night. I found the pots and pans, but there were no eating utensils in the place. When I told Darnell that we did not have any spoons, knives, or forks, he blew up, took off his sunglasses and threw them down so hard that they shattered; he started cussing, and rushed out the front door and just stood out front with his head down. I didn't know what to think or do. What in the hell have I gotten into? He came back in after a while and apologized to me for his actions. That sounded very familiar; was he not just apologizing to me for something similar just two nights ago? I felt that he was just frustrated after all that we had been through. I tried to help him feel better, tried to talk to him. There was no penetrating that wall that he had built around himself. I assumed he would come out of that mood sooner or later.

Chapter 7

We moved into a furnished one-bedroom apartment that he chose for us. Even though there were three of us in the family, for some reason he picked a one-bedroom apartment and for some reason I went along with him. "Where will Camille sleep?" I asked him. His decision was for Camille and me to sleep in the bedroom and he would sleep in the living room. This would be our arrangement until we brought a smaller bed to put up in the same room for Camille. I was fine with that; it would only be for a little while anyway. I guessed that he felt strange with all three of us sleeping in the same bed and so did I. This adjustment to a different life would take some time.

I was so excited about having my own place. It was a nice apartment; the furniture was very well made. The living room had a set made of the kind of vinyl that looked a little like leather. There were sliding glass doors and a patio off from the front room. I liked our first home, except that it had only one bedroom. I started getting the house together, unpacking everything and directing Darnell on some things that needed to be put together. I asked him if he would put a towel rack together for the bathroom. He exploded, "Damn, is this all I'm good for, just to put things together for you?"

"I'm just trying to get things together. We need to unpack and it's the weekend, the only time you can help me. You will be working all next week." I wondered, *What's his problem?* I guess he wanted me to act a certain way and I wasn't.

Time went on and we settled into our new life. I tried to find a job, but without any success. I couldn't drive and we didn't have a car. It was hard for me to find anything. After a while, I gave up and started babysitting for friends of ours just so I could have a little spending money of my own. He was not one to give me an allowance, and I was not one to ask because I felt guilty about not having a job. I felt that I was not contributing to the family, that everything was on him. I never thought that my being a housewife and mother was enough; I felt that I needed to help bring the bacon home also. It didn't matter that I kept the house clean and food cooked, managed the forty dollars he would give me each payday (which was twice a month) for food to keep us fed until the next payday. That was a feat within itself; we would be down to absolutely no food, maybe some lettuce or some bread by the time payroll came around again. I would always half everything I brought; a whole chicken would be split down the middle for two meals. A roast would be cut up for two meals. Wieners, packs of hamburger would be split and divided for two meals. These would not be your large family packs either, just your regular-size packages. These things I did to keep the family fed but I felt I was not an equal partner in the marriage. Even though every day I would play school with Camille, while playing I would teach her how to read and write and count. By the time she went to kindergarten, she was well advanced.

We had our routine all down during the week. After breakfast, she would watch *Sesame Street*, *Mr. Rogers* and the *Electric Company* while I cleaned the house and decided on what to have for dinner that evening, which was always a challenge. After that, we would play school, then eat lunch, then she would take a nap. While she was napping, I would roll me a joint (it wasn't hard to find a contact once we got settled in) and sit down to watch my stories for three hours. She would be up by then and I would start dinner. When we first arrived and got all set up in the apartment, I would get very lonely; I was missing my family a lot. We didn't have a phone turned on in the house even though there was a blue one in the bedroom. When I'd get really lonely or sad, I would go in the bedroom and pick up the receiver just hoping for a dial tone. I did a lot of my communicating with all of my friends and family through the mail. I did not know what to do with myself on some days; I would have the house all cleaned and dinner ready by 3:00 and Darnell would not get home until after 5:00. That loneliness made me get closer to him; he and Camille were my family. As long as things went smoothly, we all got along fairly well.

One day in particular, I was missing him a lot; I had smoked me a joint and was feeling a little romantic. I thought that I would run into his arms when he came in and give him a big kiss and he would kiss me back like they do on TV. When he came home, I ran up to him and reached up to put my arms around his neck. Instead of him responding, he took my arms away from his neck and pushed me away. He came into the house and said nothing to Camille or me. This action hurt me so bad it hurt my feelings and my ego. That would be the first and last time for that, I told myself and it was. I never tried to fly into his arms again after that.

Camille was still trying to adjust to him as being an authority figure in her life. Darnell would tell her to do something, and she would look to me and I would repeat it, then she would do it. This made him angry, so I talked with her and told her that it was all right to do what he asked her to. She just could not get used to him and she refused to call him daddy; she called him Darnell for years. When he would call her to tell her to do something, he would talk so rough and gruff to her. One day, he called her, not knowing that she had just come into the same room where we was. He called her name and she jumped out of her skin. "Oh man, I don't want her to be afraid of me," he said. I believe she was a little afraid of him.

One day, he and I were out on the patio while she was asleep in the house. When she woke up, she couldn't find me so she started crying. We heard her crying so Darnell decided to go to her. "I'll go see about her," he told me. I heard him tell her that it was okay, that he and I were just outside. She didn't want any part of him at all that time; she wanted her mommy. By this time, she was really crying and would not settle down; she must have thought that I had left her. She was just a little girl and all she wanted was her mommy; he could not quiet her down. I started in the house to see about her just in time to see him punch her in the belly and pick her up and throw her on the sofa. I rushed him and slugged him good and pushed him. "What is wrong with you? Why did you do that—are you crazy?!!" I couldn't believe what I saw. The look on his face was shock. I don't believe he realized what he was doing; it was as if he had lost it for a minute and got so mad and frustrated at her that he lost control. He gave me this incredible look as if to say, "Yes, what have I done?" I picked my baby up and tried to comfort her. "I want to go to bed, I want to go to bed" is all she said over and over again. He ran out of the back door. I didn't care if he ever came back.

I took her into the bedroom and she finally calmed down. "Why did he do that?" she asked.

"I don't know, Camille, I just don't know." I was so shocked, all I could do was lie beside her in bed and we both fell asleep.

He came back hours later wanting to talk; Camille would not come near him. He had been crying. I asked him why did he do such a thing. He said that he thought that she would calm down once she saw him, but she didn't and that frustrated him and no matter what he did, she would not calm down. He lost control; he talked about going to get some counseling. I was still so angry with him, I didn't care what he did. I really didn't know what to do either; it took a long time for all of us to get over that.

They say that you never know a person until you live with them. That first year of marriage was truly an adjustment period for us all. I started seeing a lot of strange behavior starting to surface with him. He had his own way of thinking and doing things different than the average person. When he went to the credit union to borrow money for a car, we talked it over, and decided that he would borrow $1,000. I just assumed that would be for a down payment on a nice car. He left that morning and was gone all day; I couldn't wait for him to get home so I could see our new car! Well, he drove up in a 1965 Buick LaSaber; it was long with a white body and green top. I was speechless for a while, I just stood there with my mouth opened. "I thought you was going to get a newer model."

"This only cost me $799, I paid cash for it so we would not have a monthly bill." He was so proud of his car. I didn't say anything else. I was starting to get in the habit of just not saying anything, just keeping it to myself. His temper was really bad at times and he really could blow and make a scene, so I just kept quiet and went along with the program. As long as I had my reefer, I was cool.

After a short while, the car started acting up; every time we turned around, something would go out on it, the starter, a hose would bust, the battery would go out, the alternator, just something with that car all the time. One day, he decided to take us for a ride. We were about ready to go out the door when his most precious tape player started to act up. I really don't know what happened; it just stopped working for some reason. He could not get the tape player to come back on. Camille and I were sitting on the sofa when all of a sudden, he picked that tape player up and threw it down on the floor; it broke into a couple of pieces. He then proceeded to literally stomp his tape player into hundreds of smaller pieces; he was just pulverizing that machine with his feet. All the time he was stomping that machine, pieces were flying everywhere.

Camille and I just sat on the sofa afraid to move; my heart was just pumping and I was hugging my daughter. When he stopped, he looked over at us and said, "Let's go!" So, out we went.

I was a nervous wreck. We got into that car and he squealed out of the apartment parking lot throwing seashells everywhere. All parking lots in that town were filled in with seashells instead of gravel. He started down the street driving just as fast and reckless as he could, turning corners on two wheels. "What's the matter with you, are you crazy? Slow down and stop driving this car so crazy before you kill us!" I was so angry with him.

This type of behavior would start to surface from time to time, not very often, but it would be there. He would be up at night sometimes alone and I would wake up and hear him talking to himself. I would listen to his conversations, they would be involving him rehearsing things he would have or should have said to someone at work where there had been an apparent misunderstanding about something. One night, in particular, I woke up to a lot of noise; he was in the living room just ranting and raving and throwing stuff. Going on and on about me always moving stuff where he couldn't find it. I had discovered that he was a pack rat and every article he would write or picture he would take that appeared in the base newspaper or even the local newspaper, he would bring the whole publication home, not one but four or five, and just stack them up in the corner in the living room. The house was starting to look like a newspaper office or a storage room for old newspapers. I would try my best to camouflage all the excess papers so our house would look like a home instead of a warehouse. That night, he was looking for something and he was talking about me like a dog. I was not going to lie there and just take that, so I got up and went into the living room. What a mess; stuff was everywhere; he had just thrown books and papers and dumped drawers, just trashed the living room.

"What are you doing, what are you looking for?" I asked.

"Why are you always moving stuff?" He informed me that he was looking for some important letter he got in the mail. But I remembered him laying it on top of one of his many piles of newspapers. I calmly went over to one of the piles, looked behind it and there was the letter lying on the floor where it had fallen. I picked it up, handed it to him and just walked out leaving him standing there looking foolish.

We lived in Florida for four years. All the times were not bad. We had good times also. I met many friends while there. My first friend was a girl from Louisiana. I was walking home with Camille from the corner store one day when all of a sudden, a car just pulled up and asked me if I wanted a ride. I had seen her before; I got in and she took me home. Her name was Mary and she had a little girl named Cherry. She dropped me off and went home to put some groceries up; she lived just up the street from me. She came back down to my house with her little girl; I got the impression that she was as lonely as I was.

We got along from the start, and so did Camille and Cherry. We talked all day long about everything, before we knew it, it was time for our husbands to come home from the base. We became good friends. She was a good cook and she taught me a lot about cooking. She also didn't take any stuff off of her husband either. When she got mad at him, she would do things like catch a ride on base over to the hospital parking lot—he worked at the base hospital—take the car off the lot and drive home to Louisiana. She was my hero; I would never do such a thing. I really don't know what kind of relationship she had with her husband, she never talked too much about that, but from the amount of times she went home, I don't think they got along too well.

Another friend I met through Darnell. He had run into a guy from Florida and they knew each other. We were invited over to their house one night; this is when I met my running buddy Faye. She was pregnant at the time; we hit it off so well, and we just laughed and talked. The men were in one room, which was obviously the "get high" room. The entrance to that room had beads hanging in place of a door, which was the rage of the day and was furnished with beanbags and a big stereo system and the room smelled of incense. They went into that room and Faye, Camille and I went into the living room and talked. I wanted to go into the other room for just a second, but I was not invited so I stayed put and talked to my new friend. She was from Canada and was a military brat herself. She introduced me to a Hispanic girl from the Bronx named Maya; she was married to a guy that was half-Korean, half-Black also from New York named Bernard. We found out that everybody got high, so we all hit it off pretty good.

After a while, my circle of friends grew and grew. We all had so much in common, all military wives with a bunch of little kids running around and there was not a time that one of us was not pregnant. We would go to the grocery store together; sometimes there would be four of us in one car all going to do our grocery shopping for the family. We'd go into the store empty-handed and come out with grocery bags, enough for four families with hardly any room in the car for the food and us and the kids. But we'd pile the food and ourselves into the car, go over to one of our houses, put the perishables into the refrigerator and hang out all day. Sometimes we would play cards, or just sit back and watch the stories and of course, someone would pull out a joint and we would start cooking and having a good time. Then the husbands would all gather together with us after work over whoever's house we would happen to be at. Dinner would be cooked, everybody would eat and the party would start.

I met a lot of good girlfriends back then; we helped each other through the hard times. I met another good friend through Faye; her name was Denise, from Tallahassee, Florida, of course, and she got high also. The three of us would have a good time together just hanging out and talking. All the friends we met all lived off base when we met them; they were all on the housing list for base units and they all eventually got nice places to live in on base. Everybody but us; my husband marched to the beat of a different drummer. He didn't want to move on base; he didn't like the idea of the military having access to any home on base. He had heard that the SP's could come into your house anytime they wanted to and he just didn't like that. I never heard of this actually happening to any of my friends, but I went along with my husband's program and we stayed off base in that one-bedroom apartment.

I decided that I wanted to have another baby and that it would be a good idea economically to have one while he was still in the service. I really don't think he wanted to have any more children at all. He already had the two from his previous marriage and we also had Camille. We had numerous discussions about another baby, but he was totally against it. My feelings towards him changed rapidly; I didn't want him to touch me anymore. I started praying that the lord would help me to have some feelings for him as his wife. We went back and forth for a year about this baby issue. For that entire year, I had to pray; I really did not want him to make love to me, not if it was not for the intentions to get me pregnant. I really wanted to have his baby; why could he not understand that, why did he not want me to have his child?

Finally, one day he gave in and I went off the pill and the next month, I was pregnant. I was so happy and so was Camille. All the time, my friend Faye stood by my side. She had given birth to a little girl and soon after that her husband had to go on tour for months. She decided to go back home to her family while he was away. I really missed her a lot. We used to have so much fun together. She was a real trip; we had all types of adventures together. I was so glad when she came back to Florida. She got a job and asked me to baby-sit for her and I jumped at the idea because that meant extra money. On her days off she would come over and we would go shopping. I was mostly window-shopping as I never had any money.

I remember on one occasion, it was almost time for Camille to start school and Darnell had brought me a sewing machine so I could make her some clothes for school. I didn't have much money, just enough to get a pattern and some material. The most economical thing to do was to buy one pattern with a lot of different outfits included inside, then buy a lot of material. I couldn't decide between two patterns because I liked both of them. I finally chose one and put the other one back. The same thing with material, I had to get the best buy for the money I had to spend. I made my decision and we went back to my house. When we got inside, Faye opened this medium-sized purse and started pulling out all kinds of material and patterns! I couldn't believe her, my girl Faye was truly a trip! Everything I had wanted but could not afford, she had lifted for me. How she fit all that stuff in her purse, I will never know.

After that shopping trip, I was always wary about going out shopping with her. One time we were at a shoe store and she just traded her old shoes with some new ones and just walked out of the store with me trailing behind her with my mouth opened. One other time, her daughter needed a winter coat and she came over to get me to go shopping with her; I made her promise not to turn into Mrs. Kleptomaniac while we were out and she promised. We got into the store and she tried a pretty coat on her daughter, buttoned it, picked her baby up and walked right out of the store with me trailing behind her once more. This was a major department store at the mall and I know she was nervous, but she wanted that coat for her baby. We jumped into the car and sped off as fast as we could. She looked over at me. I was so mad at her. "Faye, if that's what you want to do, it's fine with me but not while I'm with you." She promised me that she would not do it again and I don't think she did. If she did, I did not know about it.

Chapter 8

Before my son was born, we moved into the two-bedroom apartment that our friends Maya and Bernard moved out of when they got on-base housing. I was glad that we finally had two bedrooms. Camille finally had her own room and she was very happy. I fixed the apartment up as well as I could. Of course, it was furnished; we had not obtained one piece of furniture of our own yet and we had been married for two years at that time. I had started going over to my friend Denise's house a lot. I really liked her; she said she would keep Camille for me whenever I went into labor.

Denise was a different kind of person, in tune with the "other world." She would dream about animals all the time and could interpret her dreams or anybody else's. She dreamed about her husband's grandmother burning up in a house fire one night. She begged him to go to Tallahassee to see her; he did not take her seriously. A few days later, we got the news that his grandmother died, in a house fire. The exact way that Denise saw her in her dream; she was trying to climb out of a window. She would stay up all night sometimes because she was afraid to dream. Sometimes she would not go to sleep until morning. Her husband Ron liked to read supernatural books; she was so afraid to touch them that she would shove them under their bed with her foot. She was my spooky friend and I loved her very much.

When the time started to get close to my due date, all our friends lived on base, and we really did not know our neighbors that well. A new family had moved in next door to us and we spoke in passing. By that time, I had learned how to drive and had my license. Thanks to my friend Faye, she would let me drive her car for practice. Darnell tried to teach me how to drive, but he made me so nervous. He was an awful teacher, waiting until the last minute before telling me which corner to turn, grabbing the steering wheel, yelling at me; he was very intimidating. After a while, I refused to go out with him and that seemed to be fine with him; I don't think he really wanted me to drive.

I had a doctor's appointment one day, and he couldn't drive me back home from base after that particular appointment. I had to drive home by myself. I was a nervous wreck, my foot was shaking as I placed it on the gas pedal and it shook all the way home, but I did it! After that, I started driving by myself for practice. I gained a lot of confidence after a few months. I was over at Faye's house one day and we decided that it was time for me to get my license. I used her car to take the test and I passed! I was so happy; I called Darnell at work and told him that I had my license. He didn't sound too pleased; as a matter of fact, he was pissed! I was just going on about how I drove during the test and how nervous I was. But I passed and now I have my license. He was not enthused at all; what a damper to my mood. Well, I didn't care if he was upset, I was happy and so was Faye; we celebrated for the rest of the day. We just lay back and puffed on a few and talked about men like a dog until it was time for me to go home. Camille was in school so she dropped me off at my house just before the school bus let her off at home.

So now I was driving legally and was able to go where I needed without having to ask my husband to take me. I felt a little independent and I'm sure that after he got used to the fact that I could go to the store and the doctor or wherever, he was fine. I started driving him to work on base as the time got closer for the baby to be born.

I always referred to our unborn child as "he" or "him." Darnell would ask me why I always referred to the baby as a boy. I told him that I knew it was a little boy, I just felt it so deeply. One morning after taking him to work, I went to do a little grocery shopping. It was raining, so I had the headlights on. After unloading the car, I went about my daily duties of cleaning and cooking etc. It rained all day long; I had started to have small cramps in my back every now and then. I was five days away from my due date of June 15. Darnell got a ride home from base that day. I saw him get out of the car and walk over to ours. He looked very upset, just standing out in the rain. He came into the house, slamming the door. "Do you know that you left the headlights on the car all day? The battery is probably dead."

I wasn't used to driving around in the daytime with my headlights on. I never thought about them at all, I just got out of the car and went into the house. We didn't have any money to just go out and buy another battery; I felt bad about that. He went next door and asked our neighbors if they could give him a jump. Instead, they let us use a spare battery they had for their boat. I was really getting cramps more and more as the night wore on. I didn't tell him that I suspected that I was in labor. The contractions were not coming very regular, so I just was not sure that this was really true labor. We went to bed and I slept pretty well that night.

When we got up the next day, we took the old battery into the garage to get it recharged. Then I drove Darnell on base and came on back to the house. I parked the car in the front yard, turned to get out of the driver's seat, and as I did this my water broke. Well, I guess it's time. My mind starting ticking, what to do next? I got Camille out of the car and we went up to the apartment. I made sure everything was turned off, went into the bedroom and retrieved my overnight bag that had been packed for a few weeks. We didn't have a phone and I knew I had to call Denise to tell her that I was on my way to the hospital. I tried to stay calm for I didn't know how much time I had. My contractions had not really started coming regular. It was just the fact that my water had broke and my doctor told me that if my water was to break to come straight to the hospital. Well, I drove over to the corner store to use the phone. Sue, the cashier, was a very nice lady and we had struck up a friendship; she happened to be working there that morning. I ask her to let me use the phone to call my babysitter. She handed me the phone and I called Denise and told her that I was on my way. "Are you in labor, girl?" Sue asked.

"Yeah, I believe so, but I have to make just one more phone call."

"Well hurry up, I don't know anything about delivering a baby. Girl, you are something else. Are you driving yourself?"

"Yeah, I think I have plenty of time. I just need to call the hospital to tell them that I'm on my way."

After I called the hospital, Camille and I got into the car and off we went. I never thought to tell my daughter what was going on, I guess because I really was concentrating on doing what I needed to do to get myself to the hospital. I just drove to Denise's house and dropped her off and rushed over to the hospital. I parked in the parking lot and walked to the OB/GYN department and checked in. Once I got settled, I called Darnell at his office and told him that I was at the hospital and in labor. I had put off calling him before because he was still mad at me for allowing the battery to go dead the day before. He was not speaking to me, which was common whenever he got mad at me or was upset about something that may not have anything to do with me. He would go days and sometimes weeks without speaking to me. He would not even acknowledge my presence when we were in the same room. I would try to talk to him, but it was as if I didn't exist. I would fix dinner and have his plate of food on the table with Camille's and my dinner and he would take his plate from the table and eat in the living room. He could make you feel as if you didn't exist at times. I used to ask him to show me that switch he has attached to him that allowed him to turn his feelings on and off so well. These actions on his part were very hurtful for me to endure.

Then after a few days, he would just come back from wherever he went and would just start up a conversation as if nothing had ever happened. I'd ask him why he stopped communicating with me, what had been wrong; sometimes he would tell me, and sometimes he wouldn't. He would act as if he didn't know what I was talking about. The first time he got in one of his "dark moods" (this is what I called them) he just came home from work and did not speak to me or touch me for one whole week. I kept trying to get him to talk to me, to even look at me. He wouldn't. I was puzzled, trying to think what I had said or did to him to make him turn his back on me, his wife. I told him that I didn't have anyone to talk to and he responded, "Talk to Camille."

I used to tell him, "I'm your wife, your mate for life, if you cannot open up to me, then who will you open up to?" I would never get a response from him.

This is why I waited to call him. I figured my being in labor would change his mood, and it did. He came right over and sat with me until our baby was born. It was a very hard delivery; I had our son naturally, which was what everybody was doing back in the '70s. I also elected to breast-feed as everyone was doing that also. My main reason for that was more economical than anything else. Our son was born after eighteen hours of labor, shorter than my time with Camille, which took twenty-four hours. But more painful because of my decision to go "a la natural." I do believe, after Darnell witnessing his wife being in such turmoil for so long, that he gained a little more respect for me as a female. At least that's what he told me. I had to fight with him to even get him to be in the labor room with me. He finally agreed to be with me and I'm glad he did just so he could see what I went through in order for his son to come into the world. We named our son Stephen Darnell; my husband had picked out that name.

Stephen was a big boy and he looked just like a little man. Some babies, it's so hard to tell if they are girls or boys, but with Stephen, you could tell that he was just a little man. Everywhere I took him, people would make comments like "look at that little man." This was my son and I loved him so much. I do believe that Camille, being so young, just five years old, thought that she would have an automatic playmate in her little brother. She was very disappointed when I brought him home and he would not play with her. My friend Faye came over a couple of days after I came home from the hospital and took Camille over to her house to spend the night and play with her daughter Rachel. Faye told me the next day that she asked Camille if she missed her little brother. "No, all he does is just lays there" was her comment.

My husband was very glad to have me back home from the hospital. He would come to visit me while I was there. "When are you coming back home?" he asked. "I get up in the morning and fix breakfast for

Camille, after that, I start to clean up and before I know it, it's time to fix lunch and then after that, I have to figure out what to cook for dinner. I fixed some rice last night and she wouldn't eat it because there was no gravy. I don't know how to cook gravy."

I thought this is really funny; now he sees it's not all that easy being a housewife. The day he picked me up from the hospital, he dropped Camille, Stephen, and myself off at the house and went grocery shopping. When he got back from the store with the groceries, he just deposited them on the table and left. There I was, fresh from the hospital, with two kids, standing at the kitchen window, watching my husband barrel off down the road to work. I looked around the kitchen, dishes in the sink from breakfast and surrounded by bags of groceries. I started to cry while putting the groceries away. I felt totally alone so far away from my family. I really needed my mother at that point but she was hundreds of miles away. I so hoped that she would be able to come to Florida to help me with the new baby, but that was not possible. So, chin up and resume your duties and take care of your children.

As I said, I breast-fed Stephen for economical reasons and because that was what a lot of the young mothers on base were doing at that time. It was a great experience; it felt so natural to do this. The times I spent feeding him, especially in the middle of the night, were very special. He was a child that didn't really want to be cuddled; he was always on the move, so the only time that he was still was when he was being fed. He would just wiggle and wiggle when you would try to hold him. He was raring to go; at around four months old, he was ready to get down on the floor. He started crawling very early and was into everything! He'd crawl across the floor so fast that he would run right into the wall and bump his head every time.

I remember one day when his father came home from work; Stephen had been crawling for a while. Darnell opened the door and came in; Stephen squealed with joy and crawled as fast as he could over to his father's feet. Darnell just looked down at him with this surprised and confused look on his face. "Pick your son up and kiss him hello," I told him. "Kiss him in the mouth; that's your son."

It seemed as if he didn't know just how to take his son wanting to greet him in that way. I was beginning to put together in my mind just how deprived my husband had been of human emotion while growing up. He seemed to be way out of touch with any type of understanding of natural feelings. Very uncomfortable with the kind of family love that I grew up in.

He was an only child and I can't say that he was lonely; I really don't know if he had a lot of friends that hung out at his home. He told me of acquaintances he had all through school, but as far as being with other kids a lot I just don't know. His parents had a very strained relationship. They had separate bedrooms and did not get along too well. I got the idea that he rarely came into contact with a lot of physical or emotional love from either parent. I came to the conclusion that the reason why he talked to himself a lot was because he had been by himself all his life. I only saw his mother twice in the nineteen years of our marriage and his father three times.

The first time I met them was while Darnell was still in the Air Force in Florida. I was a nervous wreck; they were en route, on their way back from a trip to Oklahoma and they decided to swing by our house since it was on their way back to their home. Darnell had to go into town to attend a class he was taking for extra credit towards his degree. Wouldn't you know that they would show up before he arrived back home? I greeted them as best I could, knowing that we had never had any contact at all. Darnell's mother stopped communicating with him when she found out that he was getting re-married. An entire year went by without the two of them having any type of conversation. Then, out of the blue, she started writing him and their relationship picked back up where it left off before we got married. She never asked about me or expressed any interest in meeting her new daughter-in-law. Her husband seemed to be along for the ride only; I don't think he shared her feelings at all towards his son or me.

The moments after they arrived at our apartment were very awkward and tense. I was so nervous that when Darnell's father pulled out a cigarette and asked, "Do you mind if I smoke?" I said, "No, go right ahead," but I forgot to retrieve an ashtray for him. I introduced them to Camille and then excused myself to put her to bed as it was rather late when they did arrive. I was relieved to be in the bedroom with her to escape the thick air in the living room.

As soon as I returned into the living room, Darnell came into the house. Boy, was I glad to see him. Apparently so was his mother. She got up from where she was sitting and ran over to her son to hug him. I saw such love in her eyes and the way she hugged him was so touching. This confused me immensely because of the type of relationship they had in the past. She had deliberately cut him off because he had gotten married again. Now, here she was just eating him up and acting like there were never any bad feelings between them. They stayed for just a few hours and then they left to spend the night in a hotel before they started their drive back to their home.

The relationship between parents and son resumed and everything was just fine after that visit. Fine between them, but there was never an attempt on their part to include me in the family at all. I know that this made Darnell feel bad the way I was just totally ignored. Darnell and his parents had a lot of conversations about this and he told them that if they did not accept me then they did not accept him. This didn't change their minds (or her mind) about the situation. I came to see that my father-in-law was a really nice man, but I guess to keep the peace in his home, he just went along with his wife.

We went to see them once during the summer because Darnell's two children from his first marriage were visiting for the summer. I was not looking forward to this trip, but I went because he asked me to. There I was going into a home that I was obviously not welcomed in and officially meeting for the first time my two step-children. The trip over was not long enough for me; I really didn't want to do any of this. The house was just beautiful, very neat and clean. The children were very easy to get along with and they hit it off really well with Camille

My father-in-law, John Moneymaker, was very nice and welcomed me warmly. Verdene Moneymaker, however, was very cold towards me; she never once stopped moving the entire time we were there. She worked continuously washing clothes, cleaning, cooking. There was not one time that she ever made eye contact with me. I tried to strike up a conversation with her, but she was not having it. The only thing she said to me at the end of the evening was that she had changed the sheets on the bed that we would be sleeping in. Then she said goodnight and left us downstairs, Darnell, his father and myself; the kids had all gone to bed earlier. I excused myself and went upstairs to try to escape this whole day through sleep. The next day, all I wanted to do was to get the hell out of Jacksonville, Florida, and back to my home. We left around midday. I have never been back to that house since that weekend all those years ago. That was the last time I ever laid eyes on my mother-in-law also. Darnell and I had been married only two years at that time and we remained married nineteen.

The communication between Darnell and his parents continued until they got the word that I was pregnant with his child. If Mr. Moneymaker had anything to say, it was not said at that time. However Mrs. Moneymaker had plenty to say; she did not want Kevin and Kendra (Darnell's first two children) to have any more siblings. How was he going to pay for all those children etc. etc. etc.? No more communication after that, she cut him off again; as quick as she turned on, she turned off. This type of behavior sounded so familiar to me. This was the same way my husband reacted to me if I did something that he didn't like. He knew nothing about unconditional love, only conditional love. This way of loving was all he knew because this was all he was given.

During my pregnancy, Mr. Moneymaker did come over to see us for a weekend. I was four months pregnant and he was so very pleasant. I felt that he was trapped in a loveless marriage and was just trying to ride things out as best he could. I really liked him and I felt that he liked me; this visit made me feel better about my father-in-law. When Stephen was born, Darnell didn't tell his parents that they had a new grandson. It just so happened that I shared the same room with the wife of a friend of Darnell's from Jacksonville. His parents came over to see their new granddaughter. After this visit, the parents ran into Mr. Moneymaker and mentioned that they had seen his grandson (small world). Darnell's dad told his wife that he was going out to the store to buy some greens, but instead, he went to Western Union to wire us some money. I must say this at this point, because this has always been so very hurtful to me. I gave Darnell two children; we had a daughter a few years later. His parents never laid eyes on either one of them nor did they have anything at all to do with them.

Chapter 9

When Stephen was seven months old, Darnell was up for re-enlistment into the Air Force. He decided that the military life was not for him; therefore, we started making plans to leave Florida. We decided to move back to West Virginia in order for him to continue his education. The plan was to move in with my parents until we found jobs and a place to live. We would be there only until he finished his education, then we would move on to bigger and better things. I had high hopes for our future; Darnell became quite an accomplished writer and photographer during his stay in the Air Force. The sports and entertainment section of the base newspaper won a lot of awards while he was the assigned writer for these sections.

It was very hard saying goodbye to my friends; we had so much fun being together for those few years. One thing about the military is that you are constantly saying goodbye to people. My friend Faye and her husband left a few days before we did. Some of my other friends had already gone to other assignments; we were the only ones getting out of the military. My friend Denise told me that she had a dream about our two families; she dreamed that they would be going somewhere on an airplane and that we would be going somewhere in a truck. This dream turned out to be very true because, a few days before we left Florida in a truck, they got orders to go to Hawaii and, of course, they flew. So, we packed up our belongings and left Florida, bound for West Virginia

We left Florida in the month of January. We had been gone for four years and now returning with not too much more than what we left with, just an extra child. We had a few pieces of furniture that had been given to us or that Darnell had picked up off the side of the road that someone had thrown out. I tried to get him to borrow money from the credit union so that we could get some furniture while we were still in the military, but he refused. We left my hometown with a U-Haul van and returned with a truck one size up from that van.

It was a very long trip. We took a wrong turn in Kentucky and ended up in some very high mountains; they were so high up that I could look out of the window of the truck and see the tops of other mountains. I was so scared; I just closed my eyes and prayed a lot until we made it down the mountain. The journey returning home was just as long and tedious as the journey leaving home all those years before. We did the trip in two days. We got lost a lot and when we got almost home, we ran into a snowstorm in Kentucky. The snow was blowing all over the place and it was hard to see in front of us; we really didn't know which part of the road we were on. I just knew that my parents would be worried about us; we were hours late and it was getting dark outside. We got stuck on the median in the road, out in the middle of nowhere it seemed. There were no businesses anywhere and the little bit of cars that passed us did not stop.

I kept imagining us freezing to death out in the middle of nowhere, or worse, some other vehicle running up on us in the blinding snow. Finally, a truck driver stopped to see if he could help us. While he and Darnell discussed our situation, I tried to keep the kids occupied and thanked the Lord for our rescuer. The trucker left and promised that he would get a tow truck out to us as soon as he got to the next truck stop. About an hour later, a tow truck showed up and pulled us off the median. We paid him and started on our way. I kept thinking all that time, *Why is it so hard for us to get anything done?* This trip should not have been so hard, just plan things ahead of time and get in the truck and go. I was still trying to allow him to be the leader of the family, trying so hard to let him be the head, to make all the decisions.

We made it to my parents' house after eleven o'clock that night, we started our trip the morning before around 9:00 or 10:00 a.m. My parents were already in the bed when we arrived. They were so glad to see Camille and of course, they had never seen Stephen at all. I took the children up to my parents' room and they hugged and kissed Camille. Then I handed them their grandson; they immediately showered him with lots of hugs and kisses. He was just crying and looking back and forth at the both of them. I'm sure he was thinking who are these strangers my mom just handed me to? We had a few things to get out of the truck, so I left him with my parents. Camille was at home once again and was very happy to be back. My mother told me that while Darnell and I went to unload a few things that I had packed, Stephen didn't know what to do with himself. He would look at my dad and cry then take off crawling across the bed to my mom. Then he would look at her and start crying then crawl back across the bed to my dad. Back and forth he would go until, finally, he settled down in my mother's arms and went to sleep.

Thus began my life as a married woman living with her mother. Two women under the same roof can get very interesting. My only salvation was my sister Lizzie who was younger than I. She just happened to be living up the street from my mom. Lizzie was always a free spirit and moved out on her own very soon after high school. I always admired that about her. She truly had a mind of her own and did just what she wanted to do. Therefore, she was living with a young man that graduated from high school with me. He was quite handsome; I did not blame her for being with him. He and I flirted around for a very short period while I was in high school. She had written me while I was living in Florida to tell me that she was dating him. I wrote her back and told her that I didn't blame her, I knew how good he could kiss.

I would go down to her house with the kids sometimes and when I needed a break from my husband, my kids, and my mom, I would go down to her house by myself and we would party for a little while. My mom always knew where to find me. She never failed to call up to Lizzie's house after me. I had become used to coming and going as I pleased seeing how I had my own home for four years and was raising two children. I guess she still looked at me as her teenager or something. It never failed, Lizzie and I would be sitting back laughing and talking, having a few drinks when the phone would ring. "Oh no, I know who that is," I would say. Lizzie would answer the phone, and sure enough, it would be Momma. I'd pick up the phone, "Hello, Momma." I knew what she wanted.

"Your children are hungry. When are you coming home to feed them?" she asked.

"I'll be right there," I'd say very calmly into the phone.

If that weren't the conversation, it would be, "Your husband just came home from work. Are you coming home to fix his plate?"

I wanted to ask her, "When was the first and last time I saw you fix Daddy's plate?" But, I respected my mother far too much to say such a thing. As it was, I would always rush home to find my kids at the table with a plate full of food setting in front of them. I would look down at the table and up at my mother. "I've already feed them," she would say. I would be furious. After a while, I would take my kids with me whenever I went to visit Lizzie. However, that did not solve the "feed your husband" dilemma.

I was really eager to get my own place once again. The plan was to live with my parents for about a month or two until we saved enough money to find a place of our own. Of course, I had to get a job first and so would Darnell. He got a job right away, working at a grocery store in the meat department. He also started getting prepared to go back to school. He would be getting additional money for school through the G.I. Bill.

I had no idea how to even start looking for a job, I just know that I had to start somewhere. I had been apprehensive about going out to find a job since I had never really actively pursued a real job. The deciding factor that got me up and out of the house was an event that was the beginning of a change for me. I remember coming down the stairs in my mother's home and tripping and falling down a few steps. This caused my glasses to fall off my face and break. I wasn't too upset, because I knew that Darnell had been working and he could pay for the repair. When I went to him to let him know that I would have to get my glasses repaired, "I will let you have the money to get them repaired, but you will have to pay me back when you get a job," was his reply. I was so shocked that I didn't know what to say.

Then I got mad. "Don't worry about that, I will be sure to pay you back!" All I could think about was all the time I spent praying to the Lord to please allow me to get a job so I can help my husband help the family. Then he comes up with this bull about paying him back? I stormed out of the house on my way to the bus stop in order to find a job. On the way, I was so mad, I was crying then I started praying. "Lord, help me to find a job so I won't have to go through that humiliation again."

I promised myself that I would never ask him or any man for anything. I knew that I had to be self-sufficient from then on. I got on the bus and went downtown. I didn't have the slightest idea where to go. Then, I remembered seeing an ad in the paper for Manpower. I found the building where Manpower was and went inside. It was around one o'clock in the afternoon. I had no appointment but I went in and talked to the lady inside. I had no experience at anything at all. I was so unprepared for this unscheduled appointment that I didn't even take a typing test which is the first thing you would do if you had a scheduled appointment. However, by the time I left that office, I had a job at a company that supplied industrial pipes and fittings to different companies throughout the Tri-State area. I would be the new file/mail clerk. By the time I got home, she had called to leave a message as to where I was to go and what time to report the next day. I was so happy and I was just thanking the Lord for answering my prayer so quickly. Sometimes he will do that for you if it is absolutely necessary. This was absolutely necessary as I felt the need to get out from under my husband's supervision. I also needed to feel some self-worth as I didn't have a good image of myself being a mere housewife and mother.

My job turned out to be great; I had no trouble blending in with all of the employees even though I was the only black in the whole company. This fact did not and has never held me back from doing my job or made me feel different than anyone else.

I had a rather embarrassing moment on the first day around lunchtime. One of the salesmen asked me if he could get me anything for lunch while he was out. I ask him where he was going and he replied "McDonald's." Well, what did I know about their menu? Absolutely nothing, considering I had not been in a McDonald's since I got married four years earlier. I tried to play off the fact that I could not name one sandwich on the menu.

"The biggest hamburger they have" was my reply. I gave him the money and he brought me back a Big Mac. I made sure I went to McDonald's and lots of other places after I started getting paid.

I advanced pretty fast in the company I went from file/mail clerk to accounts receivable clerk in a matter of months and did a very good job. I started developing a pretty good sense of myself (just a little) through my job. Also just living day- to- day, trying to balance a job and being a wife and mother helped.

I was really eager to have my own place, especially after I got my job. I did pay my husband back for my glasses also. I did this with my first paycheck; after that I made it a point never to ask him for any money. We handled our money separately; I would determine what needed to be paid and we would go in half on the bills and what was left over on his check would be his and what was left on mine would be mine. He acted as if he wasn't too anxious to move out of my parents' house as we had planned. I asked him, "When are we going to move? I thought we would only be here a few months then we would be moving."

"Let's wait a couple more months then we can move." This became his theme song, "let's wait." So we did wait for a few more months. We found an apartment one block over from my parents' house. This apartment was on the second floor of a two-story brick house that a friend of my mother's owned. We had the second floor, plus the attic had been turned into two bedrooms. I was so happy to move into my own home at last. I was glad to get my belongings out of storage, what little there was.

We still didn't have too much in the way of furniture. Since our landlords were friends of the family, they gave us a few pieces of furniture that they had intended on giving away. We had been given a sofa and a couple of chairs. Stephen had his baby bed and my sister Lizzie gave Camille her old bed because she was moving to Atlanta. Darnell and I slept on a box spring and mattress that was also left in the apartment by our landlords.

We stayed there for about three or four months before we were evicted . The landlord wanted my husband to be responsible for the cutting of the grass, which was reasonable enough. However, the landlord would drive by the house once a week to check things out, and if he saw something he did not like, for instance, we were running late for work, and placed a bag of trash under the stairs until we got home that evening. The landlord would call and complain. If the grass was not cut when he thought it should be cut, we would hear about that. He also wanted my husband to be responsible for an empty lot that he owned next door to us. He wanted us to keep that grass cut also. Darnell offered to cut a deal with him as far as lowering the monthly rent if he took on that responsibility.

This offer was ridiculous as far as our landlord was concerned. We found out that our neighbor downstairs was having all kinds of trouble with the landlord also. As a result both families got eviction notices at the same time. We had a month to get out, so we started looking for another place to live. The time was ticking away and we had not found a new home. I was getting very frustrated with the way Darnell was handling things, as if he really did not know how to go about finding us a place. But, one day, he called me and told me that he had found another apartment just down the street from where we lived. "It's not in the best of shape, but we have to take it for now until we find something else." I went to look at the apartment; it was in an old ,old, old apartment building that I remembered when I was a child. It sat directly across from the elementary school that I attended and that Camille was currently attending. This building was a SLUM! Of course, it was furnished; there was an old sofa in the living room that I refused to sit on. They removed that and we replaced it with our sofa. Once again, we stored what little bit of belongings we had. Moved into this roach infested place that was well over seventy-five years old.

The night we moved in, I could not bring myself to stay there; all I wanted to do was to run as fast as I could out of that place and never come back. It was very late at night by the time we got moved in. I had to get out of there. I turned to him and said that I would be back then I just left. I picked up a huge stick from off the ground for protection; I don't know what good that would have done, but at that point, I did not care. I had to walk and talk myself into going back into that place and trying to make it into some sort of home for my family. I stayed gone for about an hour, then, I went back prepared to make the best of a bad situation. This I did and we lived there for about a year, constantly fighting those nasty roaches! I got so good at killing those suckers that I could see one out of the corner of my eye and swat that bug flat. Of course, I made sure I had plenty of reefer to help me along. I was just a reefer-holic if there is such a term. Everything would be just fine after I took a few puffs, and I did that quite often. Darnell and I had been getting along pretty good as long as everything went his way.

We did not have a lot of arguments during that time. We would talk a lot about us moving to Atlanta, Georgia. My sister Lizzie would write to me and tell me a lot about the city. Also, a few of Darnell's frat brothers lived there and gave him glowing reports about how much opportunity there was for blacks down there. So, we decided that would be our home as soon as he finished his education. He was attending the local university working towards his master's in journalism. I was still working at the same place and Darnell had different jobs while going to school. He never kept a job for too long; he had jobs at different stores and worked for a while at the local community center which sprung up at the start of Affirmative Action in the late '60s or early '70s. He also landed a pretty good job at the VA downtown. The only steady money coming in was from my paycheck.

After he got his master's, he decided to further his education by getting another degree in business; he did this also to continue to get money from the G I Bill. This check was steady money also, so even though he worked in a lot of different places, we did not do too bad. We started working towards our future in Atlanta; he wanted to publish his own magazine. He decided to do a sports magazine, which would be perfect, considering all the black colleges and the pro teams in the area. He started a little business on the side while we were in West Virginia. Taking pictures and developing them at the house. He had become very good at this, and had a few clients. We decided to include this in our business plan. So, not only would we have a publication, but also a photography business on the side. Everything seemed to be coming together in our minds. We named the photography business "The Miraculous Eye." He even designed a logo and had some cards printed. I was beginning to become quite proud of him. He worked very hard to get everything going and he would stay up late at night working in the darkroom he had set up in our bathroom. Everything was going fine; we just needed to move into another place.

Chapter 10

We found a really nice apartment; again, this was furnished but the furniture was very nice, so we just kept what we had in storage. We knew that we would only be in there for about another year or so. I really liked this place; it was so clean and it had just recently been remodeled. It only had two bedrooms so Camille and Stephen shared a room. It was in this house that Stephen, who was two years old, started having trouble sleeping. He would insist that we keep the light on all night and we had to make sure that the closet door was closed all the way. He would wake up screaming some nights from nightmares. Even though I liked the apartment, sometimes I would get the feeling that someone was standing behind me, especially whenever I was in the kitchen washing dishes. I would feel someone there, but when I turned around, no one would be there.

Then one night, as Darnell was getting ready to go over to the university to cover a game, he had his camera bag on his shoulder. Stephen asked me, "Mommy, where is Daddy going?"

"To the school to take pictures," I told him.

Stephen pointed behind his father. "Is he going to?" he asked. I looked at Darnell and he looked at me.

"What did you say, Stephen?" I asked.

"Is he going too?" he asked again still pointing behind his father.

"Uh no, he's not" is all I could say. This was a little strange, but I had a feeling that Stephen was able to see things that others could not. I later found out from our landlady that her deceased husband was a photographer. I have always wondered if this was who Stephen was referring to that night. He has never slept well, he has always been haunted by terrible nightmares and seeing things that no one else could see. It was always at night when he would see things. He had to have a light on in order to sleep, not a small nightlight either; the large overhead light was required.

At times, this would not be good enough; even sleeping with his father and myself would not do on some occasions. He would be truly frightened at something. At times, he would scare me, he would wake up from a horrible dream screaming for me. I would go in to him and, he would be so scared, sometimes I would take him back to bed with me and his dad. I would put him between the two of us, thinking this would calm him down. All night long, he would be popping up and looking around the room as if he was seeing something. Of course, I would not see a thing, but it was very obvious that he saw something in the room. I would watch him sitting straight up in the bed just looking around with his great big eyes so afraid. This would scare me. *What in the world does that boy see?* I would wonder to myself. Just to think that there might be some type of entity present was very unsettling. I don't know why he was that way. I know that I had a very strange experience early one morning soon after I had conceived my son; I don't know if this experience was a contributing factor to his situation, but it was very odd.

One morning, while we still lived in our first apartment in Florida, I was asleep. Darnell had already left for work. I used to have very strange dreams in this apartment, and it was always during the early morning hours that this would occur. I remember hearing Darnell leave the house. I settled back down in the bed and went back to sleep. I don't know if this was a dream, or if I was in between that sleep/awake stage. All of a sudden, my entire body became very hot and then a sudden coldness overcame me. Something grabbed me firmly by both of my feet. I felt myself being dragged; it seemed out of my bed by my feet. I felt my body being pulled right out of the bed. As I was being pulled, I thought to myself, "This is Darnell, he has come back to scare me."

But, after a short second, I realized that this was not my husband! As my body starting moving down the length of the bed, I became very frightened and held on to my pillow. I kept my eyes closed. The next thing I knew, I felt as if I was being cradled in the arms of something huge, as if I was a child. All the while, I kept my eyes closed tight and held on to my pillow. This huge whatever it was started rocking back and forth the way you would rock a baby to sleep. I felt some comfort for a second until I heard it breathing very heavily. This sound was very loud and sinister. I became very frightened; I knew in my heart of hearts that this was not a good place to be! I started shaking my head back and forth, furiously, back and forth until, all of a sudden, I was back in my bed and awake! I guess I was asleep and it was a dream, even though it seemed like I was awake during that whole experience. This has never happened to me again, but I will never forget about that morning.

I decided that the only way I could deal with that event was to accept it and go on. Now that I look back on it, I feel as if this was some type of "out of the body" experience. It was very strange but true and still very real to me to this day. Perhaps this is why my child has always been so scared at night. In fact, there are a lot of people in my family that have had lots of strange experiences during their sleeping hours with lots of bad dreams and sometimes visions. We have all just accepted that this as being something that is the norm in my family. I have one niece in particular that told me that she knows exactly what my son goes through, because she has always had very horrifying dreams all her life also. This is in addition to seeing, I suppose you could say, spirits floating around your room at night. I have awakened myself to see very faint visions of something from time to time. Especially in that apartment in Florida; I never was really comfortable in that place, especially at night.

I do remember seeing what looked like a shadow of a man with a hat on standing in the doorway of the bathroom. This bathroom was connected to my bedroom. Now that I think about it, I remember seeing this same shadow over my bed one night when I was very young. I had a candy bar and did not want to share it with one of my sisters. "The devil's going to get you if you don't give me a bite." I didn't share with her and, later that night, I woke up and saw this shadow over my bed.

I remember screaming and screaming, which is not uncommon in my family, someone was always waking up screaming from a nightmare or from seeing "something" in the night.

As for Stephen, I felt that he would grow out of his nightmares eventually. Until then, we tried to deal with him and his nightly episodes, as my younger brother Jeremy would refer to them. He also suffers with this problem and so does his daughter.

After that night when the dead photographer went to take pictures with Darnell, he and I started talking about having another child before we moved to Atlanta. I told my mother that we had been thinking about having a third child, and she looked at me as if to say "Are you crazy?" Then, she said it, "Are you crazy, with the economy being as bad as it is?" she asked.

"We will make it. This will be our last child," I said to her. I really did want to have another baby. Camille was growing up, she and Stephen are five years apart and I just wanted another baby. Camille was very excited about having another little brother or sister. She was such a good child I didn't have to discipline her too much. I believe she was born old. I mean, she always pushed her own self to do her best at anything she set out to do. I never had to make her do her homework; she would just do it. She has always been a very mature person. This does not mean that she didn't have a childhood, because she did. I believe she was so mature because the two of us were together all the time and we talked more like friends as opposed to me being the disciplinarian over the child. My mother observed us having a conversation once while we were visiting for Christmas. "You two are best friends aren't you?" she asked. I never looked at it that way, but I suppose we were. It seemed as if my children and I have had to be best friends because, as they got older and my marriage starting falling apart, we were thrown together for a lot of comfort.

Darnell and I started working on my getting pregnant, which like before did not take too long; before I knew it, I was expecting my third child. He came home one day—it was around Easter time—and announced that he wanted to take the kids and me out to the park on Easter Sunday to take some pictures. So, after church, we all went out to the park; we were all still dressed up in our Easter outfits. Darnell was equipped with his camera and tripod and rolls on top of rolls of film. I knew that this would be a long photo-shoot. He liked to take lots of slides and pore over them to get just the right one. He took lots of pictures of me that day in the park. We really had a nice time out that day and it was so beautiful; everything was in bloom and there were a lot of families out just enjoying themselves. After the slides were developed, it took us a few days to pick out the picture he liked. He told me that he was going to send the slide to a company in California that developed pictures up to the size he wanted my photo to be. This was going to be my Mother's Day gift and the size he wanted was thirty-six by forty-eight, a pretty big picture. When it arrived at my mom's house, I must say that it was a very good photo of me. I really liked it a lot; it was a closeup of me up under a weeping willow tree, and he hung this picture up in our living room over the sofa.

After a while, this picture started representing something more than just a gift from my husband to me, his wife. It became a source of uneasiness for me, as I would observe my husband sometimes staring at my picture; his stare would be intense. Especially if for one reason or another, he would be mad at me. He would get this look in his eyes that would be a combination of love mixed with hate. He would be just standing in front of the sofa staring at me in that picture. I always expected to come home one day to see that picture defaced in some way. He had lots of pictures of me throughout the house. I never realized this until I had a Tupperware party one evening and one of my guests made that observation. "Boy, your husband sure loves you, he has your picture everywhere." I knew that he loved me very much and I had grown to love him as much as I could, I felt pretty comfortable in our marriage; things seemed to be going our way. We had our future all planned, Camille was doing really well in school, Stephen was our healthy little boy, and we were expecting another baby.

It was during this time, my brother Jeremy and I decided to drive up to Detroit, Michigan, to visit our older sister Anna for a week. The plan was for us to drive up and spend a week with her, then for all of us to come back home for a family get-together. We had a really good time in Detroit with our sister. My family is so close, when we get together there is a lot of laughter and fun, a lot of love expressed for each other. We always have a hard time saying goodbye once we get together. There are a lot of hugs and kisses and especially, tears. When we got back home, there were a lot of my family members at my mom's house. I drove over to my house to see Darnell and to unload the car and to say hello to him. We had been apart for a week and I knew that he missed me. He had a class that night, but wanted to have some time alone with me. I told him that we could be together that night when he got back from his class. I told him that I was going back over to my mom's house to see my family. I wanted him to come also, but he said that he didn't want to. I believe that he was always uncomfortable around my family; I think it was the closeness that he could not get used to. He seemed to resent my spending a lot of time with my family but that didn't stop me from being with them whenever I wanted.

I left the house and started over to my mom's to spend some more time with my family, some whom I had not seen in a long time. We had a really good time eating and laughing and reminiscing and just being with one another. When I returned home, I left my kids over at my mother's house. I returned to an apartment that looked like a hurricane had gone through it. I knew the signs, Darnell had thrown one of his tantrums and the house was a complete wreck. The first thing I did was look up at that picture he had taken of me, sure to find it completely defaced. It wasn't, but there were books and papers everywhere, even out on the roof of the porch that sat beneath our apartment. I could not comprehend why he would have done such a thing; of course I never knew what he was thinking. I cleaned up the mess and left; I went back over to my mother's house and did not say a word to anyone about what I had found.

When I returned home with the children later that night, he was there; I put the kids to bed. He was sitting on the floor of a small room just off of our bedroom. This room was a very pleasant place to be as it had bay windows. I had put a lot of plants in there and more or less, turned it into a sitting room for me. I loved to open all the windows and feel the cool breeze circulating throughout the room. I would stay there for hours, reading and listening to music. This is where I found him and he had been drinking and had smoked a joint.

I looked at him. "What is your problem?" I asked him.

He returned a look at me that was pure torture. "I'm in love with a woman that I hate," was his reply. This statement shocked me, but, once I thought about it later, I knew why he said that. He loved me, but he hated how much he loved me. I believe he knew that I could not love him the way he needed me to. He was really drunk, and we stayed up all night arguing; he told me that I might as well leave him.

"You might as well leave me now. When we get to Atlanta, you will leave me anyway for someone else. Someone better than me that can give you more than I can," he said.

"Stop talking stupid like that. I'm not going to leave you!" I said back to him, really believing this in my heart; I was committed to staying with him.

"I'm going down to the courthouse tomorrow to file for a divorce. We won't make it," he said. At this point, I don't know what got into me, I started begging him not to do that, not to leave me. I made quite a scene behind that statement. All the time I was crying. I really wasn't feeling that desperate about him leaving me; however, I found myself begging him not to go. After things settled down, we made love and went to sleep.

We had been up most of the night and I was so tired when I got up. I had to go to work the next day. I got up and looked in the mirror; I looked awful! Big bags under my swollen eyes from crying half the night. I looked in on Darnell, he was sleeping like a baby. Something struck me at that moment as I watched him sleep; he looked so satisfied and peaceful. *He got what he wanted out of me,* I thought to myself. *He got me to beg for him, for his love, he tried to break me,* I thought. My begging him to stay must have made him feel in control of me or made him feel good about himself. I felt as if I had lost some self-respect; I had thrown my pride out the window and I didn't like the way that made me feel. I promised myself that I would never put myself in a position like that again. I would never beg any man to stay with me. I kept playing those scenes over and over again in my head. Not believing how I had let myself down. I eventually got over that night; Darnell walked around as if he was completely triumphant over me and I suppose he was.

Time passed and I continued to work and wait for our third child to be born, I couldn't get a feel for this child, if it was a girl or a boy. With Camille, I had hoped it would be a boy that looked just like David, her father. But I felt that she was a girl and I am glad she turned out to be a girl. Of course, I was very sure about my son, but with this one, I could not tell at all.

She was born on May 25 and boy was she a beautiful little baby; she had a head full of black curls, not a bald spot anywhere. I had been out of work a long time; she was almost a month overdue. Each week, someone from work would call to check up on my progress. "No baby yet" would be my reply. I had gone into my third week of being overdue when I started feeling small contractions. I took Darnell to work that morning and went over to my mom's house for the day. I felt better being there than at home with just Stephen and myself. I timed my contractions all day long; they were not coming too close together at that time. Camille got out of school and walked over to Mom's house and we waited there until it was time for me to pick Darnell up from work.

After we got home, I told him that I had been having labor pains all day and that the contractions were starting to come more frequently now. This didn't get too much of a reaction out of him; he never asked me how I was feeling or if I needed anything. He just took a chair out on the roof of the porch that sat under our apartment and just sat there. I went into the living room with Camille and Stephen and told them that I probably would be going to he hospital that night. Stephen was so excited; he had told me that baby in my stomach was his baby. I remember one day, he came to me staring at me very intently. "Mommy, how did you get that baby in your stomach?" I was trying to think of an answer for him when he switched his stare to my mouth. "Did you eat it? Don't eat any more babies, Mommy, okay?" I figured that was a really good conclusion he had come to, so I left it at that and told him that I would never eat any more babies.

As my contractions started coming faster, I decided that it was time for me to go on to the hospital. I got up to tell Darnell that it was time, we should start out for the hospital. So we got ready to leave. I got the kids ready while he got his camera equipment. He had intended to take pictures of the delivery; we had talked about him doing that for weeks. We dropped the kids off at Mom's and went to the hospital.

The labor was very long and painful and I had already experienced two previous labors that were very long. I was determined not to have a long one with this child, as if I had anything to do with controlling such a thing. I watched the clock as each hour ticked by; I arrived at the hospital at 8:00 p.m. on the twenty-fifth of May and was still in labor at 8:00 a. m. on May 26. I was so disgusted when I turned to the TV mounted on the wall and *Good Morning America* was coming on and I was still pregnant! When my doctor finally appeared in my room, it was like seeing my savior I felt so relieved. He examined me and looked kind of worried. "I might have to do a caesarian on you; you've been in labor a little too long for me. I will check you again after I make my rounds."

The next thing I hear is the sound of my mother's voice out in the hallway, I was so glad to see her. "You haven't had that baby yet, girl?" She came over to my bed and held my hand. This was comforting for me as I understood that she knew exactly what I was going through.

At last, the doctor came back to check me. There I was spread eagle, with his head down in between my legs. "Boy, what a head full of hair," he said. All of a sudden, instead of one head down there looking, it was three, my doctor's, my husband's, and my mom's. Never mind me, I thought, I'm just lying here in pain, go right ahead, take a good look. Finally, I was wheeled into the delivery room with Darnell in tow with his camera equipment.

Once I started pushing the baby out, he started snapping away. I must say, he got some really nice shots of our baby being born from beginning to end. Those shots are very lovely and I hold them very dear to me. I could not believe how beautiful she was—we named her Alana.

We thought that Alana was a name befitting of her beauty; all the nurses at the hospital raved about her. My baby, the prettiest one in the entire nursery! This baby girl came into the world without her grandparents' knowledge that she not only was expected but that she was even born. Darnell had elected to not even tell his parents that we were expecting a third child. I guess he did not want to go through any major changes with them.

Darnell's parents showed up in town around the same time that we had moved out of that horrible apartment into the one we lived in when Alana was born. Darnell came home one day and announced that he thought he had spotted his parents' car parked in front of his ex-wife's house. "Are you sure?" I asked him.

"Yeah, I'm sure it's their car; it has Florida tags on it."

I couldn't figure that one out. Why had they not told their own son that they were planning on coming to town? What in the hell kind of parents did he have? I believe this is one reason why I stayed with him; he seemed to need to be loved by someone. I would always tell myself that he didn't have anyone else but me. His parents had a very strange way to show love for their only child.

A week went by and their car remained parked at his ex's house. Finally, he received a call from his father one day while at work. Darnell gave them directions to his job and they both came by to see him there; they were about to leave to go back down to Florida. I just could not believe this had happened; I was both shocked and furious at their actions. I asked my husband if this did not hurt him, the way they treated him? He said that it didn't bother him. I did not, could not believe him. This had to hurt him, because it sure did me. I hurt for him. I sat down and wrote a very long letter to Darnell's father, never mind his mother, I felt that she was behind all of this odd behavior. I wanted to let him know how much they had hurt their only son and how much it hurt me. I needed to know how they could come in the same town and spend time with their ex-daughter-in-law and not their own flesh and blood? I told him that it was as if he didn't have any parents at all and that my parents treated him better than his own parents treated him. I didn't tell Darnell that I had written the letter; I just mailed it without expecting an answer. I just needed them to know how I felt.

Chapter 11

When Alana was seven months old, we moved to Atlanta, Georgia. My sister Lizzie came up from Atlanta to help us move. I felt very guilty about once more removing my children from their grandparents. Alana was so young and all three of my kids were permanent fixtures around my parents' house. But, as life goes, all things must change, and we were bound and determined to make it in the new "Promised Land" for blacks, Atlanta, Georgia. The trip down was uneventful, which for me, was a really good sign. We arrived in Atlanta and stayed with my sister and her boyfriend for about a week. This is all it took for us to find a place to live. We had saved enough money to survive on for about two months. We figured this was all the time we needed in order to get things together. We moved into a two-story townhouse that was really nice. It had two bedrooms and one and a half baths. We unloaded the same used furniture that we had accumulated over the years. We had the place all set up in about a week and settled into our new life, ready for the good times to start rolling in. I got Camille all set up in a school just up the street from the house. We lived in College Park, Georgia. This little town was not far from the city of Atlanta and also not too far from the airport. As a matter of fact, it was very close to the airport; I can still hear those airplanes flying overhead after all these years.

I felt so at home, so excited and renewed; I just felt that this was the place for us. I found a job in about a month in a corporate office of a company that owned numerous theaters, mini golf courses and game rooms throughout the south. The pay was pretty good, much more than I was making back in West Virginia. Darnell set out to find him a job until he could get his business off the ground. He worked very hard and in a few months, had published on his own the first edition of *Sports Exclusive*. I was so proud of him and it looked as if we were going to make it with this magazine.

But something went wrong. I don't know exactly what it was; maybe it was that this was not as easy as he thought. But things started to go downhill; his plans were not going exactly as he wanted them to go. He started to get despondent and very depressed, started going from job to job. Sometimes not working at all, spending all day in bed or just mulling around the house. We had to go apply for food stamps; the only income was mine, I worked every day.

One day I came home from work to find him lying on the floor in the corner of our living room facing the wall and curled up in a fetal position. When he heard the front door open and close, he simply turned to look at me, and then resumed his original position. I lost all respect for him; I suddenly felt very old and very tired. I just went upstairs and sat on our bed, which was still those mattresses that had been given to us while we were living in West Virginia. He had shut down completely. I don't know how long he stayed in that funk, but it was a long time.

He finally got himself together enough to go out and find a part-time job to bring in some extra income. We forgot all about the magazine and concentrated on just surviving. Our paychecks were just enough to pay some bills and buy a little food. I really learned how to cut corners and stretch a dollar. We had a little extra money left after we paid the bills, which went towards the purchase of a bag of reefer. Looking back on those days, we both should have taken that money and done something more positive with it. I suppose, at that time, this was the positive thing to do, so we thought. I really started relying on the stuff to make it through the day; also beer and wine. I would smoke me a joint in the morning while everyone was still in bed. This was my favorite time of the day, everything was so peaceful and quiet, very still, and the planes had not started flying overhead yet. There I'd be in the kitchen, cooking a big southern breakfast, have a load of laundry going and dinner in the crock pot just working and smoking. This was my special time and I looked forward to the mornings. The drug gave me something to get up for; otherwise I would have just lain there all day long. The thought of getting high would make me bound up off of that mattress and start my day. By the time I got everybody ready for school and daycare and myself ready for work, I was cruising, calm, cool, and collected.

Darnell had a lot of different jobs during this time trying to help make ends meet. But inevitably there would be times I would come home to find him standing in the middle of the living room when he should have been working. "What are you doing home so early?" His reply would be, "I got fired" or "I could not get along with him or her, so I quit."

"You go get the food stamps this time," I screamed at him. I was getting so tired of this way of life.

I had come to hate my job with a passion. The supervisor was a very unsatisfied female who needed either a man or woman, I don't know which one. But whichever, she needed one or the other really bad. Her main thrill in life was eating, drinking coffee, and making all of the clerks that worked under her miserable. There would be mornings that I would actually cry when I realized that it was not the weekend. I stayed with that company even though I hated it; I never knew when Darnell would be out of a job, so I endured the terrible atmosphere at work day after day.

Darnell finally came in contact with some backers for his magazine; we were both so excited. These men said they could help him get his project off its feet and in no time at all. Meanwhile, Darnell had been doing a lot of freelance work, photography, writing, and he had gotten back into developing his own pictures. It seemed like he was climbing back up that mountain towards the top. It had been a long hard road and along the way, I tried to keep my feelings for him intact. I was still relying on my drug to help me have those feelings. I would always rationalize to myself that there was bound to be something wrong with me. That I was null and void of any feelings as far as sex and closeness was concerned. I felt that I was actually incapable of feeling love and desire for a man. I would listen to the words of all those love songs on the radio and wouldn't be able to relate to what they were singing about. I felt that I needed my drug to make me feel alive inside.

Darnell started working all the time. He had so much freelance work that he was gone a lot doing interviews and photo shoots. He covered a lot of sports and entertainment events for various magazines throughout Atlanta. He even set up an interview with one of the top boxing contenders at that time soon after he came back from the Olympics as a champion. This interview was featured on the front cover of a local publication; the story and photos were very good. All this time, he still worked with his two backers on his own publication. He also landed a position on a sports publication in Winston-Salem, North Carolina. He wrote numerous articles each month for this newspaper and express-mailed them to North Carolina. My husband was a very busy man; however, not satisfied; he needed his own magazine. He became completely consumed with his work, which took a lot of time away from the children and me.

A lot of his freelance work got him into the pro games free of charge. I would always ask him to take Stephen with him to some of the games. I used to see a lot of photographers down on the floor of the Omni, which is where the Atlanta Hawks played their games. These men would have their sons or sometimes daughters down on the floor with them as their assistants. Darnell would always want me to go with him whenever he got a free ticket. I'd be sitting up in the stands by myself watching him down on the floor taking pictures. This never really was very enjoyable to me, because I was always by myself, while he would be someplace else taking pictures or interviewing someone. He never knew that I didn't like going with him to these events, because I didn't tell him. I would have had more fun if he was with me, like it was a date, or felt better if he had our son with him, showing some interest in raising him. We never had a lot of money to go out on, so I suppose this was his way of getting me out of the house. I only wished that he would have taken our son along with him sometimes instead of me so they could bond more.

On the nights that he would cover games without me, I would wait up for him to come home so we could spend some time together. He wouldn't get in until after eleven o'clock on these nights, but I would be up waiting. He'd come in and go straight to the darkroom. "Let me do this first and then I will be right with you," he would always say. "You don't mind do yo?" he asked.

"No, I don't mind," I lied. I did mind but never told him. He was always excited about seeing his pictures as soon as he got home, so he would always develop the film right away and then hang them to dry. Time would pass and before I knew it, I would be asleep.

Sometimes, I would call him from work and make an appointment for a "picnic." This is an event that called for lots of finger foods like strawberries and grapes, cheese and crackers and a bottle of wine. All of this prepared and carried up to our bedroom. It was an inexpensive way to enjoy ourselves; we would always tell the kids that we were out on a date upstairs. When they saw us preparing our tray of goodies, one or the other would say "I know what you all are doing, you're getting ready for a date!" We did this a lot. It started while we lived in West Virginia; this girl I worked with told me she read about it in some book about keeping your love life alive. This book described having a romantic picnic in your bedroom with your lover. It sounded as if it would be a lot of fun and very sensuous. I always enjoyed this time together. We would always have a joint or two, which just added to the fun. Of course, I knew that I needed that anyway just so I could have some fun.

The last time we had a picnic in Atlanta was one night I will never forget. I had asked him if he wanted to make a date for that evening. "Sure, I will even go to the store and pick everything up and fix the tray," he said. I was so impressed he was actually going to do this; it made me feel special that he wanted to arrange everything himself. I couldn't wait for that night. When the time came, he sent me upstairs to slip into something more comfortable and to roll a couple of joints. I sat on the edge of the mattress and waited. He came up with a beautiful tray of finger foods. Next, he came up with the bottle of wine and one wineglass. He laid all of this at my feet, then turned and left out of the bedroom. I thought he would be right back with his wineglass. Well, I waited and waited and waited. "Where is he?" I got up and put my robe on, started downstairs only to hear the tick, tick, tick of his typewriter. As I rounded the corner, I saw him sitting there at our kitchen table hard at work, writing an article! I could not believe what I was seeing. "What are you doing? I have been sitting upstairs waiting for you to come up and you are down here working!" He just sat there at the table with this stupid look on his face staring at me. I was so mad and hurt, I felt humiliated. "What were you thinking that you would ply me with food and drink and a few joints, and I would be all right?" I screamed at him. All I could do was turn around and storm back up the stairs. I'm sure I ate most of the food and drank a lot of the wine, and, naturally, I smoked a couple of joints. He never once came upstairs to the bedroom to offer any type of explanation or apology, nothing. It had become very clear to me that he had chosen his work over me. Why I didn't voice my opinion about the way I felt, I don't know. I just kept all of that inside, all the hurt and disappointment. We had been married for almost ten years by that time and I never told him how I felt.

His magazine was not going where he wanted it to go; the two backers turned out to be very underhanded. After a few issues had been printed, the money started getting short and the magazine was losing what little credibility my husband had earned for it. Darnell was always fighting with these two men about one thing or another, about money especially. "Why don't you take that magazine and do it yourself like you had planned a long time ago? You know more about publishing a magazine than they do. Why do you think you need them?" I asked him. It was as if he was afraid to really go out on his own again; afraid to fail so he never really tried. We continued trying to make it in Atlanta. This is a town that in order to enjoy it, you need a lot of money and that is what we did not have. We struggled a lot in that city and seemed to be under a lot of stress all the time.

My sister Lizzie was still in Atlanta at this time, working and just living the single life. She was my salvation a lot of the times. She'd come over and get the kids and me and show us the city or we'd go visit her at her place. I was so glad that she was still in Atlanta. She was still that free spirit that I admired; she had a lot of different jobs and a lot of different addresses also. If she didn't like her present job, she would simply quit and find another one. She could do that; she had only herself and a few boyfriends along the way to make life interesting. Nobody special until one day, she burst into the lobby of my workplace with a smile on her face so bright that it lit up the whole room. "I'm in love" is the first thing that came out of her mouth. "I'm in love with a man and he lives in Chicago." Her eyes were just sparkling. I had never seen her like that before. She truly was in love; it was all over her face.

The next thing I knew, she was traveling back and forth from Atlanta to Chicago. Writing letters and crying all the time because she missed him so bad. I knew that it would be only a matter of time before I would lose my sister to her man and to the city of Chicago. As I feared, this happened and before I knew it, she was in Chicago. I was pretty lonely without her, although I did have a few friends in Atlanta. The town was so large and I was used to a very small town; it was hard for me to meet people and be really close to them. I did have a lot of friends through my job, and some of my neighbors in the complex that we lived in but, mostly, it would be the kids and me.

I wanted to find a nice church for us to attend, but the five years we lived in Atlanta, I never found one that I felt at home in. Believe me, I went to a lot of them trying to find just the right one. Almost every Sunday, the kids and I would get up and go to one church after another. I did find one that we attended more than any other; however, this church turned out to be a who's who type of church. It was very large and I was used to a small church where everybody knew everybody. I could not find one that said "you are home" when I walked inside of its doors. I would get the usual cold shoulder from my husband whenever I came home and tried to tell him about the service.

"Why do you go to church anyway, what do you get out of it?" he would ask.

"It makes me feel a lot better when I go, helps me to make it through another week" would be my reply. Sometimes the air would be so thick on Sundays that you could cut it with a knife.

But this did not stop me from going to church. I had grown up in church and I wanted our children to do that also. I just could not find the right one for us. On the Sundays that we didn't go to church, I would get up and go into their bedroom and read them Bible stories or we would just talk for hours about all sorts of things. I really enjoyed this time with my children; we had a very close relationship with one another. Our conversations would be open and frank; they knew that they could come to me about anything and it would be all right. I needed to have an open relationship with my kids, unlike the one I had with my mother. My mother grew up in a different time and space than I did and I know she did the best she could, learning from her mother as I learned from her. I just modified her teachings to my way of thinking and that worked for me.

Chapter 12

One day in March, I came home from work. Darnell and the kids were already at home for some reason; I don't know why. Camille tells me that my niece Frankie, who was living with my parents at the time, had called me. I got a really strange feeling when she told me this. I couldn't put my finger on it but I started getting really nervous and tense after that. The phone rang; I picked it up, knowing that things would be different after I hung that phone up. It was Frankie. "Granddaddy had a heart attack, and it doesn't look good." This is all I remember of the conversation. I remember putting my hand over my mouth and seeing my husband observe this and I am sure, the look on my face. He left the room and went out onto the patio off from our dining room. I was in shock, this can't be happening, I wasn't sure what to do. I went out to the patio where Darnell was and told him the news, and there were no comforting words from him or any embraces. By that time in our marriage, I really didn't expect any of that from him. I had figured out that he was very uncomfortable when in situations such as these; he didn't know how to react, so he didn't.

In the days that followed, the phone started ringing off the hook with calls about Daddy. Questions, should we come now, how bad is he, who is with Mom now? My brother James, who was by then married and had a family of his own, lived in Kentucky or maybe it was Texas; he was military so I can't remember the town. He and his family were the first to arrive at my mom's side. My sister Lizzie was scheduled to come to Atlanta, as she and her by-then husband Roger had decided to move back. She was coming to find them a place to live and to scout around for jobs. Lizzie called me and was confused about whether she should go to West Virginia or come on to Atlanta. We both decided she should come to Atlanta; surely our daddy would be all right. We decided to stay positive and not think the worst. She arrived a few days later; Daddy was still holding on and was improving.

He had been in and out of the hospital so much down through the years from his drinking that we figured this was just another one of those times. He had already had one heart attack a few years before. He had also had sclerosis of the liver and had developed diabetes. All of his illnesses were a result of his alcoholism. Since he seemed to be improving, we did not see the need to plan to go home. Each day the word from home was better and better. I felt like I could breathe again and relax, go on with my life and enjoy my sister being with me. He went in the hospital towards the beginning of the week and had improved by Friday.

We got up on Saturday morning and started getting ready to go out and enjoy the day. I was upstairs cleaning my bedroom when I heard the phone ring. I bounded down the stairs only to meet Lizzie halfway. "He didn't make it, he's gone" was all I remember her saying. I turned and ran back upstairs to my room. My mind was in a fog. I put my hands over my eyes and fell on the bed. I felt as if I went blank. The next thing I remember is making my bed up, crying all the while. My sister had taken the kids out for a ride and I was home alone. Then Darnell came in from wherever he had gone. I looked up and saw him standing in the bedroom. "He's gone," I said while rushing into his arms. He did hold me; he held me tightly. I could hear and feel his heart beating loud and very fast. He loved my father very much and admired him a great deal because of my father's intelligence and his artistic abilities. He had become his father over the years and they loved each other very much.

The next thing for me to do was to tell my children that their grandfather had passed away and I couldn't delay this bad news as we had to start making plans to go to home right away. Alana was very young and didn't understand too much of what was going on; Camille took the news pretty bad, but my son was devastated. He was his grandfather's right-hand man while we lived in West Virginia and all the summers that the kids spent with my parents after we moved to Atlanta. Stephen would go everywhere with my father. Daddy had slowed down on his drinking and had retired from his job so he was home all the time and took Stephen under his wings. My mom told me about a time that she was looking for my son and couldn't find him anywhere. Finally, she looked in the back yard where my father was working on his car. My dad was a motor head, always had his head under the hood of a car or his body up under one. This is where she found Stephen; she looked out in the back yard and saw two sets of feet sticking out from under the car. One set belonged to my dad and the other to my son; I wish my dad would have lived a little longer for Stephen's sake. He was the only active grandfather he had and now he was gone. My poor son took this news pretty bad to have been so young; I dreaded telling him.

Stephen had started having trouble sleeping for a couple of weeks before my father died. This was far worse than anything I had seen of him yet as far as his sleeping problem was concerned. He stayed up all night just sitting in the middle of the floor, eyes as big as saucers; staring at only God knows what. Nothing I did for him would help. He would be screaming and his little body would be just shaking; my baby was so much more scared than usual, at what I did not know. I told my sister Anna about him and she suggested that I take him to get some therapy which I had decided to do but this was put on hold in light of what had just happened.

My sister Sandra lived in Louisiana with her family; they drove over to Atlanta and spent the night. The next day we all drove home in two cars; this was a nine-hour drive that I didn't want to take but had to. As our journey came to an end, I had no idea what to expect or how I was going to walk into that house. I somehow found the strength to go up those stairs unto the front porch and into the house. As I stepped into the front room, I met my mother coming down the stairs. She grabbed my hand and held it, rubbing her thumb up and down the upper side of my hand. Her look was so lost, so full of grief, so defeated. My mother had lost her mate, the man she had bonded with all those years ago. Now a major chapter of her life had come to a close; I could see that she was lost.

All of my brothers and sisters and their families gathered there in our home to give each other support. The feeling of grief was pretty overwhelming. Once again, we had all gathered together to say goodbye to one of our family members. Once again, cousins, aunts, uncles, nieces, nephews and close family friends rallied around each other in love. My father died on March 19, ten days from the date that my sister Leigh died, March 9; my mother's birthday is March 1. This month was turning out to be a very significant one for our family. The year he died, Easter fell in the month of March; he was buried a few days before Easter Sunday. I don't think that we realized that it was close to Easter until that Good Friday. Someone went out and brought eggs and dye so that the kids could dye some Easter eggs. While the children dyed eggs, we all sat around the table to address thank-you cards so that my mother would not have to do that. We all had an overwhelming feeling of wanting to protect her; she seemed so helpless at that point.

I remember getting up one morning and deciding to clean out the half bath for her, this is where my dad kept all of his medicine and his personal items. I didn't want her to do that so I did, thinking it wouldn't be that hard on me. At first, when I started, I didn't feel too much, but the more medicine I found, the more upset I became. There were heart patches, a box of disposable needles for his diabetes, test strips for him to monitor his sugar level, so many things he had to do each morning just to get his day started. This brought back a memory of his wake. I was standing at his coffin looking down at him and crying; a coworker of his and friend of the family's came up to me and put her arms around me.

"He is all right now. He was so sick, now he's not." This brought some comfort to me then and it brought more comfort to me standing in that bathroom. He was very sick; I realized this by the amount of medical items that I threw out that morning. My mother found me in the bathroom; I wanted to get it done before she saw me as I felt she would stop me. But she just looked in on me; "I thought I would do this so you wouldn't have to, Momma."

I picked up his dentures to throw away. "No, don't throw those away, Carol."

She reached for them and then, as if she had a revelation, "Go ahead," she said and turned to leave.

The day for us to drive back to Atlanta came around quickly. We had already said goodbye to some of my family. It was very hard to do this; we were all mentally and emotionally drained and none of us wanted to leave our mother. We all had a meeting and decided to have an alarm system installed into her house. This was not only for her safety, but also for our peace of mind. We left her and my oldest sister Janie and my niece Frankie all alone in that big house, just the three of them. That day was one of the hardest days in my life. We packed our belongings up along with some of the Easter eggs that the kids had dyed the day before and started out. As we drove off, I broke down into tears causing the children to start crying also. I knew that I had to get myself together as much as I could to make the kids feel a little better.

Darnell drove all the way back. He was a man on a mission; that mission was to get back to Atlanta by game time that night. He drove like a bat out of hell; I didn't have the strength or the will to make him slow down. I knew it wouldn't do any good; he was bound and determined to make it back to Atlanta in time to cover a Hawks game. Luckily, the good Lord was looking out for us and he got stopped in Kentucky for speeding and was given a ticket. This made him slow down to a respectable speed which put us back home around ten o'clock that night.

Once we unloaded the car and got the kids ready for bed, I remembered that the next day was Easter. I realized that there was no Easter candy in the house. I had baskets and grass and, of course we had the eggs from Mom's house. I convinced Darnell to go out and to pick up some candy for the kids' baskets. "What kind should I get?" he asked me. I couldn't think straight enough to go into any detail.

"Just get some jelly beans and some kind of chocolate candy," I told him. He returned with one bag of Skittles candy pieces claiming that was the only candy he could find in one of the largest grocery stores in the area. I was so frustrated with him; it seemed that all he thought about was himself; and what he needed to do for himself; like risking his family's life by driving down the highway at top speed in order to get to a basketball game. I was so tired that I just took the candy and fixed their baskets up the best way I could.

The next day came and I woke up after a fitful night of tossing back and forth replaying all the events of the last few weeks in my head. I got up and tried to start our life once more. How do you do that after being knocked all the way off your feet? Very slowly; a lot of praying and with the passage of time, I knew that things would get better.

I was standing at the sink in our half bath downstairs just doing my hair, not really wanting to, but knowing I had to keep functioning. Darnell came up to the door and starting talking about the problem he was having with his two so-called partners in connection to his magazine. He was going over there to tell them that it was over and he was going to tell them off and he was going on and on and on about it. My head was about to explode. I was not interested in such trivial problems; my father is dead and I am really hurting and need a shoulder to lean on. But, he could not see this; he could not see the blank look in my eyes the hurt or pain that was obviously there. "What do you think I should do?" I heard him ask me.

My head exploded. "I don't care what you do. I'm standing here not able to even think straight and you are asking me to help you make a decision. Go do whatever you want. I'm tired of hearing about you and that magazine. My father just died and you are standing there as if nothing has happened, just leave!" I screamed at him. He left. I don't know how long he was gone; I couldn't understand how he could just come back and resume life as normal after this devastating event.

After he returned, hours later, I figured that I had better feed the kids, but there was no food in the house. I drove to the store and wandered around for about an hour and a half not knowing what I was doing. In a daze, I would pick something up and then put it back on the shelf. I was not functioning at all. I think I finally picked up a box of fish sticks and a loaf of bread, that's all. I needed my husband really bad at that time, but he was too wrapped up in his wants and needs. At that point, I knew that I would have to get through this without him.

I made an appointment for Stephen to go see a therapist because he still was not sleeping well at all. I took him twice a week. I felt relieved that he would be getting some help. What I did not know was that I would be getting some help also. The therapist would talk to Stephen first and then she would call me in to talk to her. I started looking forward to these sessions; they gave me a chance to face a lot of things about myself; that was not too easy to do. These sessions also helped Stephen a lot, taught him how to face his fears by himself and taught me how to allow him to face them by himself. I found out that one of my problems was that I put myself last, and everyone else that I cared about before me. I needed to start looking out for myself and to start realizing that I counted. I started reading a lot of self- help books that she recommended which started changing my outlook on a lot of things. But, before I really got deep down into finding out about myself, the sessions ended. Stephen got better. He still had nightmares, but he learned how to handle them without my help, and learned how to accept them.

Chapter 13

I don't think I slept a complete night for about a year after my father's death. I would come home from work; my husband would be upstairs in our bedroom, which was where he spent a lot of his time lately. After a day of trying to hold things together at work, once I got home I would just fall apart. I'd break into a crying/laughing fit; it would be uncontrollable. All sorts of things would be going through my mind like, how did all of this happen? I was confused as to why and how my life had come to this. I didn't realize, at the time that I was going through a grieving process. I never got any kind of support from my husband. I am sure he heard me crying all the time, but he never once came to see about me. Gradually, as time moved on, I started recovering and feeling better.

The months moved on and we continued to struggle to make ends meet. One day, while at work Darnell called me very excited about something, I could hear it in his voice. "I received a call from the newspaper I freelance for in Winston-Salem. They want me to come work for them as their sports editor!" He was so excited, so was I. "What do you think, Carol?"

I just could not believe what I was hearing; after all this time now it seems like we will be getting a break. I didn't care if we had to move I was ready to go! "I think you should go for it," I told him.

This newspaper seemed to have a good reputation in Winston-Salem. It was black owned and was a weekly publication; they needed a sports editor for the monthly pullout that featured black college sports. He had been writing for this publication freelance for a number of years; now it seemed they needed an editor.

That evening, we both looked over the offer that was presented to him if he took the position. It sounded like a good one, better than anything he had so far and more money than he had made since we married. He decided to take it; all we had to do was wait to hear from the publisher to see when he needed Darnell to come to Winston-Salem for work. He was so happy; it had been a long time since I had seen him that happy and upbeat. "Carol, we are going to celebrate! Anywhere you want to go, I'll take you. Just name the place and we will go," he told me a few days after we were sure we would be moving. "You have stuck by me through all of these bad times; finally this nightmare will be over!" he exclaimed.

I wasn't sure as to where I wanted to go, so I asked around at work for some suggestions. One friend told me about this place that resembled a river boat that served really good food and there was always live jazz entertainment. This is where I wanted to go. All the time that we lived in Atlanta, we never took advantage of all the good entertainment that city had to offer. So, for once, I wanted to go to a nice place that I could enjoy. I got the directions from her and called Darnell to tell him where I wanted to go. It was a date! We decided to go the next evening after I got off work. The next morning, I got up and picked out a nice outfit to wear and went to work all excited and happy. The day couldn't go by fast enough for me. I had visions of the two of us sitting back, enjoying food and drinks and listening to some good music.

When he picked me up, he was slightly intoxicated. I didn't mind that much, but I started getting a bad feeling about the evening. We made it home. I got dinner ready for the kids, who were by that time old enough to stay home alone; Camille was in high school by then and Stephen and Alana were in elementary school. So we got dressed, and off we went.

If anyone has ever been to Atlanta, you would know that there is an art to finding your way around in that town. This restaurant was on the north side of town which we were not too familiar with. So, of course, we got lost. I guess it didn't help matters much with the both of us having a buzz on. I had directed him down this road that the restaurant was supposed to be on, but for some reason, he felt that I didn't know what I was talking about because he felt we had come down the road too far. He started getting frustrated and started cussing and driving wild and was just turning into a regular asshole. My bad feeling I had earlier was correct. My dreams of a nice evening were slowly but surely turning into a nightmare. We finally found the place. By that time, I was so upset and near tears, that all I wanted to do was to go home, but I didn't dare say a word. His ranting and ravings stopped when he saw the place. He calmed down and we got out of the car and walked into the restaurant.

The place was crowded with all sorts of people just having fun talking and dancing. We had to wait on our table, so we sat at the bar, which was particularly loud, but I could see that there was another part of the restaurant that was very cozy. This must have been where the live entertainment was to be. I say that, because we stayed in that place for only a few minutes. "I'm not staying here, I don't like this place, and we're leaving right now. It's too loud and there are too many people here!" We had only been there for a few minutes and he just exploded and got up and walked out. My heart sunk. I hated him at that moment. I kept thinking over and over in my head, I thought this was supposed to be my evening out, what happened to that?

Once we got back in the car, I had a lump in my throat the size of an orange, trying to hold back the tears, my heart pounding. I couldn't even look at him. Of course, I dared not say anything to him; I didn't want to get him any more upset than he already was. He looked over at me and said, "I know this was where you wanted to go, but I have a place I can take you that is much better. You'll like this place just as good." I couldn't believe him or myself for just going along with the program as usual. We ended up at this seafood restaurant not far from where I worked; I had gone there for lunch from time to time.

We went in and were seated at our table. I looked over at him, and he was oblivious to the condition that I was in. He was so satisfied; now he was where he wanted to be, someplace quiet without a lot of excitement. I felt like I was going to burst into tears at that moment. "I have to go to the bathroom," I said and jumped up and practically ran to the bathroom. Once inside, I went into one of the stalls and started taking deep breaths and tried to convince myself that this place was all right, and it was, it just was not "my place." I held back the tears, and got myself together, went back out and tried as hard as I could to enjoy my meal. I was truly glad when "my night out" was over and we went home. He never knew and I never told him what a lousy time I had because, when he asked me if I had a good time, I lied and told him that I did. So much for my therapy sessions; I was still that same person, trying to make everybody else's life happy at my expense. Not wanting to rock the boat, always wanting peace, but at what price?

We started making plans to leave Atlanta. The plan was for him to move to Winston early and to leave the kids and myself behind for a month or so in order for us to save money and for him to get the two of us a place to stay. The kids would go to West Virginia to spend the summer with my mother and during that time, we would find a place to live and I would find a job. He would send money to me each payday in order to help with the bills and whatever I needed.

The day he left, we drove him downtown to the bus station and, of course, the bus was late. Just our luck, we sat in the bus station for what seemed like an eternity. Finally, the bus arrived and Darnell got ready for boarding. He kissed the kids and me goodbye and walked over to the bus. There was a long line of people boarding, and he was towards the end of the line. All the time he stood there to board that bus, he never once looked back at his family. I kept standing there waiting to see if he was going to turn around to wave goodbye, but he just looked straight ahead. The thought struck me just then that he was looking towards the future, never turning back. I could not hold it against him for not looking back I understood exactly how he was feeling. Once the bus pulled off, I gathered up the kids and we drove back home.

We didn't have a hard time adjusting to him not being at home, because he was always gone anyway. The house seemed a little stress free as a matter of fact. We started preparing for our move, gathering boxes and packing a few things at a time. Packing and cleaning the house was easy compared to preparing to leave friends that the kids and I had made over the years. You would think that saying goodbye would have gotten easy for us. But this was always the hardest part of moving. I remember one day in particular, we only had a few more days to stay in Atlanta. My daughter's friend Cassandra came by to say goodbye to her. They both walked into the kitchen where I was cooking. "Hi, Cassandra. How are you today?" She and Camille had one of the saddest looks their faces.

"We had our future all planned out, we would graduate from high school, then go to college together, now that's all over with." They both had tears in their eyes. I didn't know what to say but that I was sorry. They turned and left the kitchen. I felt like a dirty dog. What could I do? This was going to be a good move for the whole family. I had not realized how hard this was going to be on the kids. I knew that once we got all moved and settled that everything would be all right.

The company I worked for gave me a going-away dinner at one of our hangouts. I walked into the dining room and there sat all of my coworkers and to my surprise, my little sister Lizzie. She and her husband had been back in Atlanta for about a year and we had hooked back up again. Now, it was my turn to leave her. I looked around the table and saw my friend Vera. She was one of my good friends, a good ole country girl that I loved very much. She always knew when I was down and out. I would tell her about some of our money problems, my worries and fears. She would always try to cheer me up. There was a song that she would sing to me when I was especially down and out. She said it was Darnell's and my theme song and she would always sing a phrase from this song it went "Even though we ain't got money, I'm so in love with you honey," she would sing this to me to try to cheer me up. Little did she know that what love I did have for him was dying little by little.

There was my birthday buddy, Patricia; we shared the same birthday and her mother, who had died of cancer, was named Carol also. I guess we kind of attached ourselves to each other. We seemed to connect; maybe it was because we had the same birth signs, but we got along very well.

Then there was Lois, one of the most beautiful black women I have ever known. She had, as Richard Pryer would say, "skin like a Hershey bar," long beautiful hair down past her shoulders and she stood at least five foot nine. She was a very sweet girl and we became lunch buddies. Now, going out to lunch with her was always an adventure. We looked like Mutt and Jeff, her so tall and me, standing five foot one and not too thin. I must say that I grew into a nice-looking woman, but beside her, it was pretty hard to notice me. Even though I was a married woman, I still liked attention, which I would get whenever I wasn't with Lois.

I remember, one lunch hour in particular, we drove over to a car dealership to talk to a salesman that had sold Lois her car. This man was a pretty nice-looking young black man. As we approached him, he was looking straight at Lois. I don't even think he noticed me until we got right up on him. "Hello, Lois. How are you today?" He was just smiling at her then he noticed me. "Who's your little friend?"

Little friend, little friend! I thought. That's how I felt around her, like her little short plump little friend. After we left the car lot, I told her that I was never going out to lunch with her again. We laughed about that, because I told her that every time we went out together. She was a very sweet person and not at all into her good looks, very genuine. I knew that I would miss her a lot; we had become really close.

After dinner, we all gathered in the parking lot to say a final goodbye; everyone had tears in their eyes. The best way to do this was quickly. We all hugged each other and got into our cars. The toughest goodbye was to my sister; we held each other for a long time and told each other "I love you," then we parted. I know I cried all the way home and through the night. We would be leaving in two days; Darnell was expected home sometime the next morning.

When he arrived, I heard the front door open around 5:00 a.m. I got out of bed and walked to the top of the stairs. There he was entering the house; he looked up at me and practically ran all the way up the steps, he embraced me so tightly. I could tell by that embrace how much he missed and loved me.

A few hours later found us packing up the U-Haul and saying goodbye to our neighbors. We got up the next morning and started off, he in the truck and the kids and I in the car following him. As with my husband when he left Atlanta on that bus, I never looked back. I was very glad to leave Atlanta and looking forward to our new life in North Carolina. This was a five-hour drive from Atlanta to Winston-Salem, North Carolina, and also to many drastic changes to come.

Chapter 14

Winston-Salem, a much smaller town than Atlanta, represented a new beginning for my family; we all were very excited and curious about this new place. We checked into a motel that Darnell had found just down the street from a storage place he had rented for us to store our furniture until we found somewhere to live. We did have a little more furniture by then, a queen-sized bed for us that my friend Vera had given me, the younger kids had a bunk bed that Darnell had purchased and Camille still had her bed that Lizzie had given us all those years ago. Must of the furniture that we had was given to us. Darnell and I had been married for thirteen years; I felt we should have had more to show for our union than a bunch of rag-tag furniture. I don't think that my thoughts were too unreasonable, but maybe I was wrong. After we got the kids all settled into the motel, the two of us took the truck to the storage unit and unloaded the furniture, turned the truck in and returned to the motel, we ate, and went to sleep. The next day we would be driving to West Virginia to drop the kids off for the summer.

When we returned to Winston, I was so tired that all I wanted to do was to go the rooms that Darnell had rented out during his solo time in Winston while we were still in Atlanta. He had found some rooms for rent in a house not too far from the newspaper where he worked. These rooms consisted of a bedroom, a kitchen and bath. All I wanted to do was to go there and get some rest. We went and got some takeout chicken and ate it in the car while he drove me around to show me some of the town. I didn't want to see the town; I wanted to go to sleep. It seemed as if he was stalling on taking me to this place. After driving around for what seemed like hours, we finally pulled up in front of this two-story brick house. It was a rather large house and there was an elderly lady sitting on the front porch. He introduced me to Ms. Bertha, who seemed pleasant enough. We went inside and up the steps. There was a large bathroom at the top of the stairs, and down the hall were two doors, one on the left side of the hallway and one to the right. We entered the door to the left and stepped into a dimly lit bedroom, off to the left of the bedroom was a kitchen. I walked into the kitchen; there was a table with one chair, a refrigerator, sink, and no stove. "Where's the stove?" I asked.

"There is no stove, but there is a microwave, but it doesn't work all the time," he said. It's a good thing I had the presence of mind not to store my electric frying pan and crock pot.. "The refrigerator doesn't work all the time either," he added. I found out that it didn't work but about eight to twelve hours out of the day, so we couldn't buy in bulk.

I walked back into the bedroom. I didn't want to lie on that bed; as tired as I was, I didn't want to do it. Especially when I saw a roach crawl across the bedspread. I was speechless. Why had he brought me to a place like this? Surely he could have found a better place for us to stay, seeing how it would be at least a month or two before we would be able to move. But, by this time, I was used to his way of doing things. I knew what I had to do, I had to hurry up and get me a job and find us a nice home to live in. I realized that in about a week's time, he had just left me up in that place for days on end without use of the car. I started walking out just to keep from getting bored; I don't know how I was supposed to find a job without the use of a car.

About that second week, I told Darnell to let me have the car for a few days; I would take him to work, and then get out to try and find me a job. I got a hold of a map of the city and started venturing out, looking for some employment and at the same time, trying to find us some place to live. We both tried a few apartment complexes at first, but were turned down time after time because we didn't have a long work history in Winston-Salem. It was at this time that I started turning to God in earnest for help. I had to find a job and I had to get out of those rooms!

Each morning, I would get up, take my husband to work then come home to start my ritual of reading the Bible, praying, then looking through the newspaper for employment and a home. The employment came first as I interviewed with a lot of different temporary agencies for about two weeks in a row. Finally I went to one temp agency that sent me on an interview with a local trucking firm that was quite prominent in the area. The vibes I had received so far on my interviews were all negative; however, the vibes I got from this interview told me that I had the job. I felt so confident; I had come a long way since the first job I interviewed for all those years ago at Manpower in West Virginia. During this time, I had also been in contact with a landlord about a house. This rental ad appeared in the newspaper for a couple of weeks. Every time I finished praying for God to guide me to a house, I would pick up the newspaper and that same address would pop out at me. I started calling the number in the paper every evening until I reached the owner of the house. This gentleman was from India and apparently owned a lot of property, a very busy man and very hard to get in touch with. Finally, I had set up an appointment to meet with him one afternoon. I had no idea where the house was or how to get to it being that I was constantly getting lost in the city. I consulted my map, which by now was getting very tattered, but I found the neighborhood and the house. It was a three-bedroom house on a nice street in what seemed like a very nice, down-to-earth racially mixed neighborhood. I wanted that house; it had a very large front yard and a smaller back yard with a driveway. After living with Darnell all those years in furnished apartments and such, I never dreamed that I would finally be living in a real house. I was determined to get that house somehow.

The evening we were to look at the house came around. I directed Darnell to what I thought was the house we were to look at. In that neighborhood, a lot of the houses looked alike and there were a couple of houses on that same street that had for rent signs out front and I parked in the wrong driveway. We waited and waited but, no sign of the landlord. We were getting discouraged and about to leave when I looked two doors up the street and saw the house I had looked at briefly a few days before. There were people in the front yard, a woman with two children and a man that appeared to be Indian. "Darnell, there is the house up there, that's the one we need to be at," I said pointing up the street. He looked up at the house and the people in the front yard.

"We might as well turn around and leave; those people probably have already rented the house out to that family." His tone sounded so defeated. I got hot, mad and sick and tired of that defeated attitude of his.

"You can turn around and leave if you want to, I'm going up there to talk to him!" I screamed at him. I got out of the car and marched right up the street to meet the landlord. I walked right up to him and introduced myself to him. "Mrs. Moneymaker, I have been waiting to meet you. Don't worry, I will give the house to you; you have been very persistent with your calls. Just let me get rid of these people and we will talk some business." I looked around and saw my husband coming into the front door. I introduced him to the landlord and he showed us the house. I told him that I would be starting a new job very soon; I had not really gotten the job yet, but I was confident that I would get it. He was a very nice man and seemed to have a lot of faith in us that we would be good tenants.

We signed papers a few days later and paid two months rent in advance. I was so relieved that we would be out of that place we had been living. The day we were to move in, I learned that I had been hired at the trucking firm. I felt blessed: a new home; a house, not an apartment; and a new job all in the same week. We went to the storage unit and loaded up all of our belongings and moved everything into our home.

I had about a week before I was to start my job. We were in between paydays and our money was running kind of short. I would go to the grocery store and buy a little food; I would eat just a little and save most of the food for Darnell. I spent that entire week cleaning the house and trying to unpack boxes by myself and get the house in order. I figured that I could get most of our belongings unpacked and the house in order before I started my new job the following week. We had been sleeping on a mattress for days. I wanted Darnell to help me get things in order but he seemed to be consumed by his job. In the evenings, he would come home late and would continue to work while I busied myself around the house. I began wondering if he was going to lift a finger to help me at all. I finally had to start an argument that weekend to get him to put all the beds up in the house and to help me put up curtain rods so I could hang curtains. As for everything else, I finished by myself. I started spending a lot of time by myself. I really missed my kids, but they would not be home until almost the end of the summer.

I remember one evening, at home after I had gotten the house all in order, I was outside in the front yard. I still couldn't believe that I was actually finally living in a house with my own front yard. I was standing there staring at a huge tree in our front yard wondering what type of tree it was when Darnell came out of the house. I was feeling so good and I had the feeling that we had "arrived," that all of the searching for the life we had dreamed of was all over. I was very content and satisfied when I heard these words, "Yeah, this is a good stepping stone for a while. We will stay here for a few years and then we will move to another city to see what I can do there."

I couldn't believe what I heard coming out of his mouth. There was no way that I was going to move again. For years, it seemed that he was running, running from something or to something. He seemed to think that he could go from job to job, place to place continuously until he found whatever it was that he was looking for. "Have you ever heard of the word commute? How could you even be thinking of moving to another town when we have barely moved in here yet? I refuse to move another time. The kids and I are not packing up and moving from city to city, following you while you chase whatever it is you are after or whatever it is you are running from. You can move wherever you want to, go wherever you want to, but the kids and I are staying here. I cannot and will not pack the kids up and follow you around the country while you try to find your version of happiness. So you will just have to commute back and forth. The children need some roots set down somewhere, and they don't have any. You have roots and so do I, a place we remember growing up and seeing the same faces; a place called home that we can go back to every now and then. They don't have anyplace that they can call home. This will be that place. Everybody needs roots and our kids do also." He had nothing to say after that; he knew that I was serious.

My first day at work was like any other first day at any job, you don't know anybody and I was the only black on board. Every job I had held in my adult life never had a lot of black employees; as a matter of fact, there were times when I was the only black employee on board. Some blacks would come and go but never stayed. I have always stayed put at my jobs because I felt that I had to in order to keep steady money coming in. Anyway, that first day, Darnell and I were down to a jar of pennies. Most of these pennies were from what I had saved since we started planning our move. I figured we would divide them up equally and make them last until one of us got paid. Instead, he rolled the pennies, which came to about fifteen dollars; he gave me about four and kept the rest. Once more, I was silent and did not voice my opinions about the money split. We both worked on the same side of town, just minutes away from each other by car, so I would drop him off on the days he didn't need the car and I would go on to work. I trained for about two week before I was on my own. One thing I must say about myself is that I never meet strangers; I just walked right into that office and claimed my space. I got along very well with everybody there. I do believe, however, that some of the employees were not used to working closely with any blacks, so it did take a while for some of them to warm up to me. One man, in particular, did not speak to me for an entire year. He would see me in the hallway and walk right past me without even acknowledging my presence. I would try to speak to him, but after a while, I started giving him the same type of treatment. I just dismissed his presence, which I learned how to do very well by way of my husband. My presence had been dismissed by him enough times during our marriage that I had lost count. Besides this man, I really liked my job and all the people there.

I worked in the same office as the dispatcher who was also a female, our boss was a female and, of course, the receptionist was a female. Everyone else was male, all of the drivers were male, but a few women came on board later on. All the drivers had to come up to our office in order to get their routes for the day and since I paid them, I got to know them pretty good. Most of the drivers were white, good ole country boys, but all were pretty nice. I did encounter a few that I had to make respect me when their paychecks came up short.

"You cheated me out of some of my money this week," one driver told me over the phone.

"No one cheats anybody out of anything around here. Perhaps there was a mistake made on your pay. If so, we will correct that mistake but I don't cheat anybody out of their money," would be my response. There were a lot of times that I had to really come down hard on some of the men. I earned a reputation among some of them as being a real mean black woman. I just spoke what was on my mind and did not mince any words either. I could do that at work better than I could at home, however.

One day while at work, I was still training with the girl whose place I was to take. A very handsome black man poked his head through the dispatch window to talk to the dispatcher. I looked up and spoke to him; he was a very pleasant sight to see after seeing so many good ole boys. I smiled and spoke to him and he spoke back. A few hours later, I heard my trainer on the phone saying, "Yes, she is married and so are you." I figured it was that driver making inquiries about me and my trainer set him straight.

Meanwhile, back at home I was very lonely and spent most of my evenings alone watching TV. Darnell was either at the office or covering some sports event. I couldn't wait until my kids came home. We had run out of our supply of reefer and didn't know enough people well enough to get a contact. On the weekends, we would drive out and go through some neighborhoods to try to pick something up, but most of the time the sellers would have other drugs, which we did not want. We decided to quit, just like that; we both felt like smoking was getting a little old and so were we. It was really risky and scary going out in those places doing drive-by purchases. Sometimes we would get taken and when we got home, there would be pencil shavings or something that looked like reefer but wasn't in those small packages. We decided, because of my husband's position, that it would be a good idea if we just chilled on the drug.

All the time we were discussing this issue, I was really afraid; afraid because I felt that I would not be able to stay with him without some help from my friend "the joint." But, I was growing tired of getting high all the time and I suppose, I was growing up a little. Looking around my house at all the used furniture, realizing that all those years we spent money on marijuana, we could have spent it on some nice furniture. All those years and all that money; I felt ashamed and disappointed in myself. I had to admit to myself that while I was doing that drug, the thought was always in the back of my head, and I could have used that money for the family instead of my head. There were lots of times that I felt so guilty, but I always pushed those guilt feelings aside. I rationalized in my mind that I needed the marijuana in order to be with my husband and to cope with my life. Now, God had put us in a position where we had to make a decision. We decided to say "no" and, surprisingly enough, it wasn't all that hard to stop. I know I did miss getting high, but there was a change going on inside of me; I really was tired of getting high. But now how was I going to cope with my problem of not being able to "feel"? I had myself convinced that I had a real problem in that area. I started making sure I had plenty of wine around the house. I had replaced one drug for another.

Chapter 15

I started seeing that black driver more and more on the job. It seemed as if he would make a special effort to come up to the drivers window each day at the end of his run. Sometimes, I would just happen to answer the phone and he would be on the other end. Every time I would pick up the phone and he would be on the other end, we would start a conversation. He started telling me how pretty I was and how intelligent I seemed to be. I really started looking forward to seeing him after a while. I was lonely and really liked the attention I was getting from this man. Meanwhile, at home, my husband was ignoring me; it seemed as if he was married to his job. I would fix myself up as nice as I could, and I never got a compliment out of him. There was no conversation between us except what was going on at his job. The sex, not lovemaking, was very brief. I would always go to bed before him and be asleep, when he would come get in the bed and expect me to perform for him. No foreplay, no kissing, he made me feel like I was his whore instead of his wife and lover. Meanwhile, back at work, this other man was paying me compliments and making me feel very desirable. I was falling for all of those nice things he was saying to me. Loving all the attention I was getting from him. But, also knowing that we both were married, I did not dare think of this harmless flirtation as anything but that, a harmless flirtation.

My home life was falling apart, I was falling apart, and I felt that while we were living in Atlanta that my husband had put me on the back burner. I don't know where I was now, maybe in the oven, out of sight. Then, one day after work, I was walking across the parking lot to my car. I heard someone call my name. When I turned to see who it was, there was my driver coming towards me. My heart started pumping fast; I didn't know what to do. I had become very attracted to this man and I had confided in one of the girls in the office about my attraction to him. I hadn't gotten a real good look at him, just from across the room, but he seemed to be pretty good-looking. Now, he was coming towards me. "Please let him be really, really, ugly up close" was my prayer. Because, if he wasn't, I knew that I was in trouble. The closer he got to me the better he looked. Just my luck, he was very muscular, he had a body that wouldn't quit and he had the nicest smile, beautiful straight white teeth, his skin was the color of creamed coffee. A very handsome and buffed black man, he looked so strong and so sexy. When he got close up to me, I had to back up; I felt such a sexual pull to this man that I had to move my body back away from him. I had never had such a feeling before in my life, not even when I was high. All I wanted to do was to jump on that man; you could feel the electricity between the two of us all in the air. My body was jumping, to coin a phrase from the Frankenstein movie, "It's alive, it's alive!" We stood there and talked for about forty-five minutes. All the time, he couldn't take his eyes off of me. It was as if he was feasting on me with his eyes; he couldn't keep them off of me, and I couldn't keep mine off of him. "I know that this is wrong, but I am very attracted to you. I think about you all the time and I want to be with you," he told me still staring into my eyes.

"I'm very attracted to you also, and if you had come to me at any other time in my life, I would send you away." I could not believe what I was saying, but I really wanted him, at that moment, to take me in his arms and just hold me. These feelings I was having felt so good to me; it had been years, almost a lifetime since I had a man look at me the way he was at that moment. All of a sudden, I got really scared. What was I doing, what was I saying to this man?

"I've got to go," I told him, all the time backing away as fast as I could.

"I want to be with you," he told me. "Please think about it."

I couldn't respond to him, I just turned and walked away, my heart pounding as fast as it could. I was in a daze, driving to Darnell's job to pick him up. He got in the car. I felt so guilty; I could not believe I had said all those things to another man. I decided that I would not talk to Alex again. That was his name, Alex Murray. I had to bury these feelings some kind of way.

The next few days, I tried avoiding answering the phone and tried to be out of the room when I felt he would be coming in from his route. But, as luck would have it, I picked up the phone one day, and it was him on the other end. All my reserve melted, all the strength I had summoned to fight these feelings just disappeared. I was in a mess. I had to do something; somehow I had to focus on my marriage, my husband, my family. Each night that we were home, I gave Darnell every opportunity to pay attention to me. I gave him all kinds of hints that we needed to put romance back into our relationship. I would walk around with just a small amount of clothes on in front of him—nothing, no response, no nothing. I would try to cuddle with him on the sofa at night; he was not the cuddling type unless he wanted some, and then he was all over me. I would snuggle up close to him and he would not respond. One day while he was driving us home from work, I just looked over at him; I stared at him for a long time. "Do you love me?" I asked. I was looking at him very intently; he barely glanced over at me. "Do you love me?" I asked him again.

He cut his eye over at me. "Yeah" was all he said. Oh, God, please help me; I felt like I was in a war. I was fighting against these strong feelings that I found myself having for another man and fighting to hold on to the little feelings I had for my husband. I felt as if I was being torn apart on the inside.

The time came for us to pick the kids up from my mom's house. We planned to leave right after work. I wanted to be all packed so that we could just leave straight from work so we wouldn't have to drive through the mountains at night. Of course, that did not happen. After he picked me up, he went to the liquor store and bought a bottle, then we went by the house to load the car. By the time we got on the road, he was on his way to getting drunk. He got all turned around in town; it took us an hour to get out of the city. I wasn't feeling that well; I had been experiencing pretty bad cramps and my head was hurting. I had told him that I could not see too good at night because I needed to change my glasses. This is another reason why I wanted to leave as soon as possible; I would not be able to drive at night and I was also afraid to drive in the mountains.

I don't know what had gotten into him. He drank almost that whole pint of whatever he had brought and we were nowhere near our destination. I took the bottle away from him and made him promise not to drink any more. He promised and we drove on into Virginia. I started to cramp pretty bad and asked him to stop at a store so I could buy some pain pills. We pulled up to this store and I got out. As soon as I stepped into the store, he pulled off. Where in the world was he going? I purchased my pills and went outside to look for him; he was nowhere in sight. After about five or ten minutes, he pulled up with a drink in his hand. I was furious at him; I insisted that I drive but he would not give up the steering wheel. We took off; he was driving like a mad man, reckless and fast. We got into West Virginia and it started raining but I don't think he noticed because he did not decrease his speed. It started to get foggy; he drove faster, weaving in and out of traffic. He started talking to himself and yelling at the cars in front of him to get out of his way. All I could do was pray and try to convince him to slow down, but he wouldn't. It was only by the grace of God that we made it to my mother's house in one piece.

I was so glad to see my children and my family, my mom and my sister Janie; my baby brother Jeremy was there also visiting our mom. Darnell was obviously drunk when he entered the house. I was so mad and embarrassed I couldn't look at him. He had cornered my brother in the kitchen and was talking a mile a minute. When he got like this, there was no shutting him up; he would go on for hours, which is what he did. I tried to rescue my brother; it was obvious that he wanted to escape Darnell's barrage of words, but with him like this you couldn't get a word in edgewise. I just went to bed; all the fight to save my marriage had just been killed on the drive up. I felt as if I actually hated him; all

I thought about was Alex. Believe it or not, he continued to drink the next evening, knowing that we would have to drive back to North Carolina the next day. I was so mad at him, when we loaded up the car that day; he had a major hangover. This meant that I would be driving all the way home by myself I thought. We left my mom's home late that day and I drove most of the way to North Carolina. He slept most of the trip. Every time I looked over at him, sleeping his foolishness off, I felt like I hated him even more. It started to rain when we got deep into the mountains; I was a nervous wreck. The trip going back was all downhill and I was not used to driving down any mountains, especially mountain roads heavily populated by tractor-trailers. Just because I worked for a trucking company didn't mean that I was used to driving down mountains with them in the rain. I was petrified riding the breaks and seeing trucks in the rearview mirror coming straight for me with their horns blowing.

We made it out of West Virginia and Virginia with me driving; he finally woke up and took the wheel. I spent the rest of the time trying to convince the kids that they would love our new home and the town. They seemed very uninterested in even trying to get into what I was saying. We made it home in one piece and unloaded the car. I couldn't get a good reading as to how the kids liked the house; I guess we were all just very tired.

The next day, I went to work; all I wanted to do was to see Alex. I did not hear from him for a few days; he had been given a long-distance run to Florida. I went home and tried to get the kids settled in our new home. We went out for long drives; I tried to show them the city, tried to force them to like it. I still had a lot of guilty feelings about having to uproot them once again. Nothing I did made them feel better about the new move, especially Camille. I decided to give up; they just had to get over it.

I got to talk to Alex after he came back from his long run. He wanted to see me, and I wanted to see him. We planned to meet behind a building just down the street from where the office was on the next Saturday, which was only a couple of days away. What was I doing, could I do it? I wasn't sure that I had the courage to meet him. When

Saturday came around, I was a nervous wreck. I had planned on going in to work that morning—this is what I told my husband—and I did. Alex and I had planned to meet around one o'clock in the afternoon. I left my job an hour before time. I chickened out, I just couldn't meet him. All I kept thinking about was what would I do if he wanted to kiss me? The only man that I had kissed in years was my husband. What would it feel like kissing someone else? To be truthful about it, I had not really been kissed by my husband in a long time. When I would drive him to work, he would get out of the car, lean back in for a kiss, he would just place his lips on mine, not really kissing me, just placing his lips on mine, for me to kiss him. If that were not the case, he would ram his tongue all the way down my throat and practically drown me. "Don't kiss me like that!" I would say to him, all the while wiping my mouth; those kisses were always too wet. Even though I had not had a good kiss in years, I was still not ready for another man's embrace or kiss.

That Saturday, I left work, picked my kids up and took them to the mall. Camille could see that something was very wrong with me; I was so preoccupied with not meeting Alex. I knew that he would be waiting for me and that I was not going to show up. I felt bad, knowing that he was behind that building, anticipating our meeting, but I just could not bring myself to do it. Even though I wanted to be there, wanted to be with him, I was afraid. If I went through with this meeting, it would change my whole life. I knew that seeing him was wrong, very wrong; it was a sin. So, I spent the entire weekend wondering what Monday would bring. I decided to end things before they began.

Of course, the next day at work, I received a phone call from Alex. "Why didn't you come? I waited and waited for you."

"Alex, I got scared. I don't know if I really want to go through with this." I said those words not really sure if I meant them.

"I just want to talk to you, that's all. Please met me for a few minutes this evening after work." I gave in and agreed to meet him in the same place. I worked late and drove to our meeting place and there he was. We got out of our cars and walked towards each other.

"All I want to do is take you in my arms and kiss you," he told me.

"Please don't, I'm afraid," I told him, all the while feeling that war going on inside of me. Wanting him to kiss me, but not wanting it all at the same time. He reached out and took my hand. I thought he was going to kiss me, but he honored my request, which impressed me a lot. We talked for a while, then he hugged me and we left.

I didn't see or hear from him for a few days as his new routes took him out of town for days at a time. Meanwhile, at home, I was trying to sort things out in my head. I had become very confused; I needed some space, some time away from Darnell. I told him this one evening as he had been noticing that I was preoccupied for some time now. I hinted that I had a lot on my mind and that I needed some space from him so I could sort things out. I guess, what I was asking him for was to not be my husband for a while. To please let me be, just long enough for me to set things straight in my mind. Instead of giving me what I asked, he panicked. After I had summoned up the courage to tell him to back off of me for a while and to please be patient and understanding with me, he did just the opposite. I went outside to be alone; I needed to be alone in the worst way. He followed me outside; he had tears streaming down his face.

"Will you at least let me see the kids when you leave me?" he asked. I looked at him not believing, but yes, believing what I heard. His defeatist attitude once more assuming the worst at all times.

"Did I tell you that I wanted to leave you, or did I just ask for some space?" I got up from the stoop I was sitting on and went over to the car; I needed to be away from him. He got up and followed me. I sat up on the trunk of the car and as soon as I sat down, he was all over me. Kissing me and hugging me so tightly that I could hardly breathe. I felt as if I was being suffocated, physically and emotionally. It was as if he had not heard or comprehended a word I said. Instead of giving me some space, he held on that much tighter. All I wanted to do was push him away from me but he wouldn't let go. I felt like screaming "What is wrong with you? Can't you understand English!" That night was the first of many long nights we would spend together in a lot of pain.

That night also pushed me all the way into Alex's arms. We agreed to meet early one morning near some office buildings. He was on his way out of town. He retrieved his truck and drove out to what would become one of our many meeting places. I was waiting for him in my car. He slid into the passenger seat and looked me deep into my eyes. Before I knew it, our lips were touching and we were involved in a very deep and passionate kiss.

"I have wanted to do that for a long time," he told me. I couldn't talk, couldn't say a word for a minute.

"I was afraid to kiss you. I have not kissed any other man but my husband in years," I told him, all the time thinking that the world would come to an end if I did kiss another man. It didn't and I liked it; I liked the way his strong arms felt as he embraced me. I liked everything about him and I felt as light as a feather.

"I want to make love to you," he told me. I wanted him to so we agreed on a time and place. In a few days we would be together in a hotel room. He said that he would make all the arrangements. We both left our meeting place that morning to start our jobs. From then on, I was in "la-la land" constantly thinking about our meeting that morning and what it was going to be like to be with him again.

Things had kind of gotten back to normal at home, with Darnell working most of the time. School had started and the kids were all settled in the neighborhood. I didn't really get that space that I asked my husband for; after that night, I tried to make it seem as if everything was fine with me when it really wasn't. Darnell seemed to center his well-being around me; I felt responsible for his happiness, and I will never forget how desperate he was that night in our front yard. How it seemed as if his entire world would come to an end if I left him. So I decided to try to pretend that everything was just fine between us.

I told him that I was going over to a friend's house for a Tupperware party. I had worn my hair down that evening and had put on a black sundress. Alex and I met at the hotel. He had gotten the key and gave it to me earlier in the day; I was to go to the room first and wait for his knock, which came about thirty minutes after I had arrived. I let him in and we embraced each other. As usual, I was a nervous wreck, kissing was one thing, but what we were about to do was entirely different. We sat across from each other at a table in the room for a while and talked.

The conversation was very easy, very light, just questions about each other's life. He was staring at me with such passion, this made me feel very desirable and pretty, and he reached out and held my hand. One thing led to another, and before we knew it, we were in bed.

The way he made love to me was very gentle and very caring, not urgent and needy like when I was with my husband. Alex made me feel as if he was giving me love; not taking it from me in order to live like Darnell made me feel. When Alex embraced me, he did it so gentle and it made me feel safe and protected. Darnell never really embraced me when we made love and when he did; it was more like a vice grip for life, not a loving, giving embrace. After that night, I was completely gone, my mind and body were whirling and whirling in passion. I felt wonderful, as if I were in love.

When I returned home that night, Darnell was sitting in the den at the table, facing the entrance to the room working diligently with his head down. I walked in and stood right in front of him. This was a test, I thought to myself. Alex and I had sweated every bit of curl out of my hair, so I braided it on one side, a style I would wear occasionally, I would brush all my hair over to the right side of my head and start a braid going from front to back. It was quite becoming and a quick and easy style. I stood in front of him, not realizing at the time that my dress was also on backwards. It was a plain sundress that scooped in the front and back; the only difference between the front and the back was the seam of the dress was to be worn on the back, not the front. I stood there and lied to him about the Tupperware party and what I had ordered; he never once looked up. I turned and walked away from him and from my marriage. He never noticed that my hair was different or that my dress was on backwards.

From that moment on I went headlong into my affair with Alex. We met whenever we could, either at our meeting place behind those office buildings after hours or a motel room or in the park not far from my house. I fell in love with this man, never thinking about him having a family or about how I had turned my back on my husband. All I knew was that this man made me feel like a teenager again and at the same time like a desirable sexy woman. There were times when we were together that we could hardly bear to leave each other. Holding hands and not wanting to let go.

"You are getting under my skin," I told him one night.

"You are already under mine," he said.

Where my husband left me feeling undesirable, Alex made me feel sexy and desirable. Where my husband made me feel as if I was his whore, there for his pleasure only, Alex made me feel as if I was the love of his life. I stopped trying to make my marriage work, didn't care anymore. I still was a good mother, just not a good wife. I started neglecting and treating Darnell as if he didn't matter any longer in my life. He was always at work, so it wasn't very hard to sneak away to be with Alex. He started calling me at home and we would talk as long as we wanted to. He started calling me so often that my youngest daughter started recognizing his voice over the phone. I remember one day, Darnell was at home and the phone rang; it was Alex. Alana answered the phone. "Mom, it's for you, it's that guy again." She sounded so innocent. I sprinted to the phone.

"He's home. Call me later," I whispered to Alex. We talked for a little while just to keep the suspicion down. I believe that Darnell knew that something was going on, but what, he could not say.

I remember the phone ringing one day and, by this time, I had become very jumpy whenever the phone would ring. I tried to be cool going to answer the phone; he followed me into the living room and stayed there the entire time that I was on the phone. Of course, it was Alex. I tried to play it off as cool as I could. Darnell was looking at me, staring at my mouth, at every word I said. I was talking to Alex as if he was one of my girlfriends, he finally caught on and we ended the conversation.

To say that I handled that affair with ease was not the case at all; I was jumpy all the time, lost a lot of weight and broke out with pimples on my face. I was always covering my tracks, lying and rushing around to meet Alex, being with him for only a short time, when I wanted to be with him all the time. Rushing home, taking a shower before Darnell got home from work; he would get home each night at least by nine or ten o'clock. The worst part of this affair was being with Alex and then, a few hours later, in bed with Darnell; this was pure torture. Being with the man that I wanted to be with and felt as if I needed to be with, Alex. Then, a few hours later, I would be with my husband, whom I was supposed to but did not want to be with. He would come to bed and want to have sex with me. I didn't want to, but to keep him from suspecting things, I would have to give in to him. Afterwards, I would lie in the bed and cry. I felt like a prostitute, being with two men in one night. That was just not me at all, but I did it and felt awful all the time. How could I continue to do this? The whole situation was pulling me apart; I felt as if I was going out of my mind. What was I going to do? I knew that my relationship with Alex was a no-win situation. But, for selfish reasons, I didn't want things to end.

Chapter 16

My relationship with Darnell was a mess; I could see that he was trying as hard as he knew how to figure out what in the world was wrong with me. On our anniversary, he took me out to a nice restaurant that featured jazz entertainment. I didn't want to go. A few years ago, yes, but now it was too late. We made reservations for around seven o'clock. Even though my husband was an educated man, he had no concept of the way things worked when you make reservations. We arrived at the restaurant and were seated at the bar. He immediately got upset. *Time for a scene,* I thought. One thing about Darnell, he didn't mind making scenes in public. He asked the hostess how long was the wait; she told him about thirty to forty minutes. I could tell by the look on his face that he was about to blow. He turned to me and said, "Man, what's going on? We had reservations, our table should be ready." I started remembering our night out in Atlanta and decided that I was not going to leave this time.

"Reservations mean that we get the next table that comes available, Darnell. Just sit here at the bar and have a drink and relax please."

After we were seated at the table across from each other, I had a hard time looking at him; he just sat there and stared at me all night. I was really uncomfortable, as I always had been with him just trying to look so deep in my eyes that he could absorb me or something. The music was nice and the food was good, but he knew that something was up with me. He told me later that night on the way home that I acted as if

I hated him. He wanted to know why I would not look at him from across the dinner table that night. I had no answer for him; I just wanted him to hurry and drive home so the evening would end.

My treatment of Darnell drove him up the wall; I suppose that's a normal reaction. I spent most of our marriage trying as hard as I could to act as if all was well. Now, all of a sudden, I'm treating him as if he is a leper. He was starting to not care about himself, not care about how he looked or smelled. He stopped bathing and stopped eating, he wore just anything to work. I was embarrassed to be seen with him. His behavior became very strange; I tried in a nice way to tell him that he needed to bathe and to dress better. He just didn't care; he started losing a lot of weight, so much that his face and eyes were sunk in. I started feeling guilty because I knew that my affair and my treatment of him were the cause of all of his misery.

He asked me out one night, just the two of us for dinner. I didn't want to go of course, but I did. As usual, it was torture and I didn't have a thing to say to him. I had completely removed myself from him and I didn't want to talk to him or even try to make small conversation. That night after we got home, I was in the kitchen cleaning up; I had cooked dinner for the kids before we left. He came into the kitchen and stood behind me.

"Why won't you love me?" he asked. He had a few drinks that night at the restaurant and a few more after we got home. The scowl on his face told me that I was in trouble. He grabbed my shoulders and started shaking me. "I want to know why you won't love me!" he shouted. He started slapping me in my face.

I tried to get away from him, but he pushed me up against the stove. There was a pan of cornbread sitting on top of the stove. I picked the pan up and tried to hit him with it. He grabbed it away from me; there was cornbread everywhere. As he turned to set the pan down, I tried to run out of the kitchen. He grabbed me and threw me down on the floor and started hitting me with his fist repeatedly about the head. All the time repeating that same question "Why won't you love me, why won't you love me?" He was straddling me and I couldn't get up. Amazingly, the blows did not hurt as I thought they would.

He got up and I tried to make a run for it. Before I could get away from him, he grabbed me by the leg. I was crawling across the floor, trying to get to my feet. He dragged me across the floor, opened the back door and threw me out in the back yard. I got to my feet, not believing what had just happened; I just stood there not knowing what to do. I heard the front door slam and the car pull off.

I went back in the house and started cleaning up in the kitchen. I had no idea what he must have been feeling behind my treatment of him. But I know that I felt totally violated by him. I had hurt him by not responding to him for months, he wanted to hurt me, and the only way he could do that was by using physical force. I had never been attacked or beaten before. The only way I can explain the feeling is of violation; I felt completely helpless under his physical strength.

The next day, I couldn't stay in the same house with him. I didn't sleep that night, just tossed and turned. When I woke up I got dressed and Camille and I went for a long walk; I knew she had heard all the commotion from the night before. We talked about it and I cried as we walked all through our neighborhood. When we returned home, Darnell was in the back yard sitting on the back steps crying. Classic guilt I suppose, he couldn't look at me when he apologized, and he told me he would never do anything like that again. I guess I accepted his apology because I felt so guilty myself for what I had been putting him through. It took a long time for things to get back to the abnormal way things had been for the last year.

Even though I felt as if I was in love with Alex, I wanted the affair to end, but I didn't know how to release myself from him. Fate stepped in; he told me that he was accepting a job in another town and that he would be leaving soon for training. My heart dropped; even though I saw this as a way out, I still didn't want to let go of him. He told me that he was leaving his family behind and that they would be staying with his in-laws. He confessed to me that he and his wife were not getting along too well and that she did not want to move with him. It was a possibility that, after training that he would be working in another town in North Carolina. He told me that he loved me very much and that he wanted us to remain close to each other, that he would come home every chance he got to see me.

He left for about two months' training and we saw each other as often as we could. He even wrote me letters and mailed them to my home. Darnell was oblivious as to what was going on; he was never home, so I felt safe with Alex's letters coming to the house. I was always the first one home and would retrieve the letters hours before he got home. We only had one car and I drove the car myself, so I felt safe that he would not be home to get the mail. All this time, Darnell was in a deep depression and still not caring about himself. I truly wanted to end my affair and try to patch things up between Darnell and myself. He was slowly but surely being destroyed by this thing. He would go out driving, sometimes all night. One morning he didn't come home and, for some reason, I knew that he was in jail. That's the first place I called and sure enough, he had been picked up for DWI. I found out where my car was and had a girlfriend of mine take me there to pick it up. Then I made arrangements for bail for him and went to work. I was really disgusted with him and tired of him acting as if he had no kind of sense at all.

Memorial Day came around and the kids and I packed up to go to Mom's house for the holiday. I was glad to hit the road, still feeling torn about my relationship with Alex. Knowing in my heart that it had to end, also knowing that all I had to do was to ask God to help me. Many a time during prayer, I was tempted to ask God to help me, but I never did. Not until I fell on my knees at my home church and cried out to him to save me from myself. After I got up, I felt that a change was going to come but I just didn't know when.

You know the saying that God answers prayers in his own time; well, his time came quick. The next day, we went back home, all of us dreading to walk back into that house. I opened the front door and it was completely silent in the house. The back door was opened and I looked out to see Darnell sitting in the wooded area behind our house. He would go to the woods quite often and sometimes take a chair and just sit there talking and fussing to himself. Fussing about me, telling the trees things that he should have been telling me. I never knew how he felt about a lot of things that pertained to me or to our relationship. He would never verbalize his real feelings when he got mad at me. I would always have to sneak around and listen to the numerous conversations he would have with himself to find out what he really thought.

When he realized that we were home, he came into the house. What a pitiful site he was. He looked as if he had not slept for days and he was dirty and was crying his eyes out. He grabbed the kids and just about squeezed the life out of them. They retreated to their bedrooms immediately; he looked at me and just broke down harder. "I thought you wouldn't come back," he said. He grabbed me and held on to me tight, his embrace felt so "needy," as if he would die if he let me go. I felt so bad that I had put him through this hell he was in. He smelled really bad; he looked like a homeless person that had been sleeping outside for days. I burst into tears and ran to the bedroom. I started seeing just how much damage my affair and the way I had been treating Darnell had affected him. I'm sure that he didn't know about Alex, because I had been pretty careful about covering my tracks. I supposed he just thought the reason why I was treating him so bad was because I didn't love him anymore.

I decided, while sitting on the edge of our bed, that I would write Alex; that would make me feel better. I started the letter; I knew that Darnell had retreated to his sanctuary in the woods. I began the letter by telling Alex how much I loved and missed and needed him to come home. Then, I couldn't think of another word to say. I realized that I didn't mean those words I had just written and that it was over between Alex and me. That Alex was not the solution to my problem. I became distraught and balled the letter up and threw it in the trash can that was in our bedroom. I just about cried half the night away, finally falling into a fitful sleep.

The next day, I was standing at the full-length mirror in the hallway just outside of our bedroom getting ready for work. All of a sudden the bedroom door opened and he rushed out and threw a piece of paper at me. It hit me in the face. I knew what it was; my mind went back to me throwing the half-written letter in our trash the night before. Why had

I been so careless when I had always made sure that all evidence of Alex had been carefully destroyed in the past? As he threw the paper at me, he walked past me and shouted, "Now I know, now I know!"

Chapter 17

For the second time in my life, I felt that incredible weight lift off my shoulders that I didn't even know was there. I felt so relieved that he knew. Now I had nothing to do but to go in the den where he was and talk to him about it. I was amazed to see how calm he appeared to be; I sat on the sofa as he stood and faced me.

"I can't say that I blame you for being with someone else, I feel mostly responsible for what has happened. I know that I drove you into someone else's arms. I must say that a weight has been lifted off of my shoulders. I don't know how long this has been going on, but I do know that it seems to have been for some time. You really had me puzzled, Carol, though sometimes I would feel that you had someone else and then, other times I wasn't sure. So, what do you plan on doing about this?"

I could not believe how calm he was and I wasn't quite sure how to begin. "I feel a weight lift off my shoulders also; I had gotten at the end of my rope. Those things that I said in the letter you found, I realized were not true, that's why I threw the letter away before I finished it." I had a very hard time looking at him; guilt was taking over me. "I have decided to end the relationship. When I went home this weekend, I prayed for a release from this affair, and now it has come. I just have to tell him that it is all over. He is not in town right now and I cannot get in touch with him until this weekend."

This was too easy; I kept telling myself he is too calm. But I was sure of one thing, he did know that he had pushed me away by his actions.

He told me that he loved me and that he didn't want to lose me and could we try to make a go of it? I told him that I was sorry that I hurt him and that I would try to make things work out with him. I finished getting dressed. I believe that I was in shock, then the realization of what I had been doing with another man, the guilt that I felt and the sorrow over hurting Darnell came crashing down on me. I was a wreck for days until the weekend came around and Alex got back in town. I called him on the phone at his in-laws', hoping that he would answer; he did. I told him that Darnell had found out about us and that we would have to end things. He didn't want to accept that, he wanted us to still see each other.

"I have fallen in love with you. Carol, please don't do this to us," he pleaded with me.

"Alex, I have to, this can't go on. I can't go on like this, especially now that he knows. I have to try to rebuild what little relationship we once had and move on. I'm sorry, but it has to be this way. I'm sorry, Alex." Then I just hung up. I felt bad ending things between us the way I did but that was the only way I could at that point.

The kids started calling me at work a few days later reporting strange behavior from their father. "Mom, he lays around all day crying and recording all this love music over the tape recorder and then repeating these phrases over and over into the recorder."

I listened to the tapes one evening. They were kind of scary, and he would repeat things like, "Carol and I have a strong marriage. She loves me and I love her. We will be together forever." He would say this over and over again between sobs.

I also remember hearing over the recorder something that made me know how upset he really was. Apparently the Avon lady came by to see if "The lady of the house was in?" I heard her voice and then his.

"No, no, no, she is not in. Go away." He was shouting at her at the top of his voice.

I knew that his calm attitude was too good to be true; he was going to start to act up, I was sure of it. I believe he went through a lot of different emotions during that time, hurt, betrayal, frustration, regret and the main one, which surfaced and stayed, was his anger. He started showing up on my job asking to talk to me in private; I would take him into our break room and he would start with the constant barrage of questions.

"Who is he? Did you love him? Did he love you? Did he make love to you better than I did?"

I got so sick and tired of his questions that I looked at him one day and told him as we sat across from each other in the break room, "Listen, my relationship with this man is over. I thought about telling you who he is, but to be honest with you, it's none of your business. Who he is, what we did, how we felt about each other, it's none of your business. What I did was personal, for me, I needed it at that time in my life. Now it's over. If we are expected to make it, we have to move on and not dwell on the past."

I truly felt this in my heart. After going over all the time I was with Alex, I knew that our relationship was something that I needed in my life; I was starving for love and attention, tenderness and companionship. Everything I should have been getting at home but was not. I looked him straight in the eyes and told him this.

"None of my business," he said. "Okay." He simply got up from the table and left the office.

I felt bad about how I ended my relationship with Alex; after all, we had been together for well over a year and it just didn't seem fair for me to just call him and end things on the phone. I agonized over these thoughts for days before I finally picked up the phone and called him. I told him that I needed to see him, that we had to put proper closure to what we had. He agreed and so we met for the last time and went for a long drive. We talked and I explained to him why I had made my decision to end things. He understood, but still didn't want to let me go. It was time for us to part after we talked for about two hours; he took me in his arms and kissed me deeper than he ever had before. Saying goodbye was very hard, but I knew I had to do it.

The next few weeks were horrible. The weekends were spent with Darnell constantly wanting to talk about my affair, and the nights, some were calm, but some were filled with him ranting and raving about me and my infidelity. There were nights when he would come home drunk;

these were the most frightening. One night, he went on a rampage, marching around the house screaming and raging and throwing mud and rocks and even his shoes at the bedroom window where we slept. It was very scary, I would lie there praying that he would pass out in a drunken stupor or just go away. Then there would be quiet for about thirty minutes, like he had left the premises, when all of a sudden the raging would start again. He would come into the house and into the bedroom. I would lie there as still as I could, pretending to be asleep until he left the room. I woke up one morning after one of his rampages and looked out of the window. Every home in our neighborhood had rural mailboxes at the curb all mounted in the ground and surrounded by cement; our mailbox sat on a metal stand. I looked out my window to see the yard littered with clumps of mud he had thrown at the house the night before and, to my amazement, the metal stand and mailbox twisted and bent and almost pulled out of the ground. That sight was more than scary; if he had that much rage inside, what would he do to us or me when he was on one of his drunken rampages?

Another night, my premonition about the picture that he had taken of me years ago, came to life. I was in bed and he came home drunk as usual around midnight. He started talking to himself and then throwing things around. He burst into the bedroom and turned the light on. He was breathing hard and looking at me as if he wanted to kill me. He had that picture in his hand, he took it and threw it at me, then he stormed over to the bed and jerked the picture up. "No, no, that's not good enough," he muttered while grabbing the picture and leaving the room.

I don't know what made me get up out of the bed, but I followed him through the house, all the time trying to get him to calm down. He was like a madman, he went into the back yard and got a can of gasoline we kept for the lawn mower. I didn't know what he was going to do. He threw the picture down on the ground and doused it with the gasoline all the while looking at me with this murderous scowl on his face. He took a match and set the picture on fire. I knew that was what he wanted to do to me. Why didn't I call the police? That's a question lots of women would ask, I suppose. But I didn't, I just pleaded with him to calm down; I was afraid that he was going to set the house on fire. He just looked at me and walked over to the water hose and put the fire out after he was sure the picture was destroyed, then he left the house.

To say that I was shaken up is an understatement; I closed and locked the back door only to turn to see my house in a complete shamble. I also discovered our wedding photo torn up and in the trash can. I knew that I had to leave him, that he had turned into a dangerous man. The next day I walked around in a dream state, not believing what had happened the night before. He had come back home and was sleeping on the living room floor, face down with his bottle lying next to him. When he woke up, he came to me like a whipped puppy.

"I don't know what got into me last night or all the other nights. Please, if you would give me another chance, I know that we could make it. I wouldn't blame you if you left me right this moment."

I decided to stay with him. My very best friend since the seventh grade, Alice, used to tell me whenever I called her crying about something Darnell had said or did, "You're a better woman than I am."

I would say, "No, maybe I'm just a fool." I believed the latter was true. I really did want to try to make a go of things with him.

We started attending church and Sunday school regularly, the entire family. Darnell and I both on separate occasions had made appointments to talk to our minister seeking some help and prayer. We both had forgiven each other and ourselves for all the hurt in the past. Our future looked bright and our entire household had settled down. To celebrate, we decided to go on our second honeymoon later that summer. I took the kids to my mom's for a few weeks and returned home so that Darnell and I could start out on our "honeymoon at the beach." He had made all the arrangements and would not let me do anything. I was very impressed indeed.

The day that I returned from West Virginia, I was real tired but I needed to go to the post office to get some stamps. I was the only driver at that time, because Darnell had his license revoked for a year. We drove to the post office. I don't know if it was because I was so tired or if it was just an accident, but when I drove into the parking lot of the post office, I drove right over a curb; I just didn't see it. I knew that the force of the bump I felt when I drove over that curb damaged the car.

We got out of the car and looked under it. There was oil pouring out of the oil pan onto the ground. I looked at Darnell, and that old familiar anger crept back in his eyes. He just looked at me, threw his hands up and walked away from me, leaving me there all alone. A couple happened to be in the parking lot at the time of the mishap; they came over to me to ask if I needed help. I know that they had seen Darnell walk off from me. I told them no, that I would be fine, so they drove off

It was getting dark and my husband was nowhere in sight. I knew I had to do something, so I went to the nearest phone booth and started handling things. I made several phone calls, arranging for a tow truck to come pick the car up. I had called a friend of mine from work whose husband was a mechanic. He agreed to fix the car for me the next day, so I had the car towed to his garage. Meanwhile, Darnell had come back talking to himself and acting a fool, stalking around the phone booth glaring at me. We were to leave for the beach the next day and I'm sure he figured I had wrecked the car on purpose so I didn't have to be with him. I called my sister and her husband to come and pick us up.

When they arrived, it was obvious that there was a lot of tension in the air. My sister Lizzie and her husband had moved to the city just a few months before. It seemed that we followed each other from city to city. Her husband had gotten transferred to the area through his job and they decided to move to Winston to be close to family. Darnell said that he would stay with the car to make sure it got towed to the right garage. Lizzie and Roger took me home. As soon as I got in the car, I burst into tears. I was so embarrassed; my sister and her husband seemed to have a blessed relationship, while mine seemed to be from hell. I couldn't say too much on the way home, I just thanked them and got out of the car and went into the house.

Darnell never came home that night. I don't know where he slept or if we would be going to the beach at all. I called the garage and my friend's husband told me that he would have the car finished by the end of the day. I finally got a call from Darnell, asking me if I still wanted to go to the beach with him. I really did want to go, but not with him; I said yes I did. I told him that the car would be ready and that our neighbor was taking me to pick the car up. He was home when I returned from the garage acting as if nothing at all had happened. I also pretended that nothing had happened; I believe we both wanted this to be "the week" that would mend our relationship.

Chapter 18

We set out for the beach the next morning, both in good spirits, driving down the road listening to oldies but goodies and anticipating the fun we would have. That week was lots of fun, daily early morning walks on the beach. Breakfast out on the balcony that overlooked the water. Darnell had a dozen red roses waiting for me in our suite of rooms. It was just lovely; we got drunk a couple of nights playing drinking games. We didn't have one fight or misunderstanding that entire week.

The day we were to leave, I woke up to an empty bed; Darnell had slept in the living room on the floor, a sure sign that something was up. He woke up and was strangely quiet for the rest of the morning. We had little conversation as we packed the car up and drove off. I was sorry to leave, to go back to reality; it had been a wonderful week. I noticed that as we got closer to home he became more and more withdrawn. When we got almost a block from our house, he made me stop the car; he got out and stormed off in the opposite direction. I tried to call out to him, but he just took off leaving me to drive the rest of the way home alone.

So much for the honeymoon, I thought as I parked the car and unloaded it. I was puzzled and confused; he didn't come home for hours, after I had gone to bed. I woke up to hear him having his usual conversation with himself. He was outside sitting on the side of the house just fussing about me. He didn't realize that the bedroom window was opened and I could hear every word he was saying about me.

"Yeah, she don't care about me, she never tries to initiate any sex with me, always waits for me to start. She sleeps with her back turned to me…." and he was going on and on and on about all the things I did wrong according to him. Then I heard him accuse me of wrecking the car because I was looking at that man that was in the parking lot of the post office.

"He probably was her boyfriend." Well, I had just about heard enough of him and his paranoid thoughts. I got out of the bed and crept around the back of the house and caught him in mid-slander.

"Why can't you be man enough to say this to my face? Why do you have to tell the air and the trees what you have to say instead of me?" He was so shocked to see me standing there with my hands on my hips wearing nothing but my gown. He couldn't say a word so I continued. "First of all, I am sick and tired of you putting me under a microscope, examining every move that I make, every word that I say, what position I sleep in, every man that I look at. It seems that everything that I do is directed against you. I am trying as hard as I can to make this marriage work and every time I feel as if we are making some progress, you do something to send us a step back. I hate you for what you are doing!!" I said this at the top of my lungs all the while balling up my fists and whaling away at him. He had stood up by this time and was moving towards the back door to go into the house. He looked like a kid that had gotten caught with his hand in the cookie jar. I was furious; the whole week at the beach was a waste.

I was so hopeful all the time we were there; he seemed to be having such a good time; now I know that he was miserable. I began addressing each issue I heard him bring up about me. "First of all, I don't initiate sex with you because I don't like rejection which is what happens whenever I try to initiate things. I sleep with my back turned to you because I like to sleep on my right side; I'm sorry if the position just happens to put my back to you. As for the man in the parking lot, I've never seen him before in my life. However, unlike you, my husband, he and his wife did offer to help me while you went off and sulked like a baby." With that being said, I turned and went to bed; of course he slept in the living room.

I went to work the next day and pretended that we had a wonderful time to everyone all the while knowing that Darnell's phobia or whatever it was that was wrong with him had messed everything up. He had called me at work and asked me to meet him at this sub shop that we liked to eat at. Not only did I not want to pick him up, I didn't even want to see him. When I got off work and arrived at the sub shop, there he was with gifts in hand; I couldn't even look at him. When we got home, he opened all these bags he had. He pulled out a bottle of wine, some flowers, a couple of sandwiches and a card apologizing for his actions. I had a collections of cards from him down through the years; all of these cards contained words of regret for treating me one way or the other. They didn't mean a thing to me, just one more to add to the collection.

Over the next few months, we struggled to get along. I started drinking more and more and eating more and more. He started staying away from home all the time. I looked at myself in the mirror one day and what I saw I didn't like. I had gotten so fat; I knew that I had put on some weight, but I felt like my face still looked good. Then I saw a picture of myself that was taken while visiting my sister and I didn't like what I saw. There was no way I was going to continue down that road, so I started on an exercise plan and changed my eating habits.

Just a week into my new lifestyle, I received a letter from my husband. He had come by my office and left a letter in the driver's seat of our car. When I got off work, I found the letter and sat in the car in the parking lot to read it. He told me that he was no longer attracted to me because I had let myself go. That he could not believe how fat I had allowed myself to get. That he had started staying away from the house on purpose because he didn't like what he saw. He also had the nerve to tell me that he was so turned off when he was with me that he had paid someone to give him a blow job one evening.

I couldn't believe what I was reading. *That coward,* I thought, *he had to write a letter to tell me this instead of telling it to my face.* I was so hurt, a realized that I had gotten fat and I realized that I needed to make a change. There are ways other than by letter that he could have conveyed his feelings to me. I told him this the next time I saw him. He stayed away for two days, then he finally called me on the phone and we had a long talk. I let him have it; I told him if he had been home long enough, he would see that I had been working out and that I had dropped a few pounds. I felt wounded at that time; I was trying as hard as I could to stay with him, to build some type of life with him, but day by day, he was tearing that life down.

Things would never be the same; he had gotten a job at a reputable newspaper in the next town about thirty miles away in the sports department. He was starting to make more money and I guess I figured we might just get along better if we didn't have money problems. His hours were from three to eleven, which meant that we didn't get to see each other too much. He had two days off in the middle of the week. This meant that the kids and I were always together in the evenings. We had our own agenda without Darnell and on the two nights that he was home, there was a lot of stress and strain between all of us. Camille had gone off to college by then, so it was just me and the other two kids.

I believe that the affair I had caused some very serious problems with Darnell's mind. I had begged him to go seek some help, to talk to someone, but he refused. However, I knew that he was in a lot of emotional pain still from what had happened. It had been well over a year since my affair was over and he still had not really forgiven me.

A couple of weeks before Christmas that year, he came home from work; he had stopped off and had something to drink. I woke up to hear him fussing and throwing things. I'd had enough of that mess, so I got up. Why did I do that?

"What is your problem?" I asked him. He was standing in the middle of the den; he turned and looked at me.

"You'd better go back into the bedroom before I hurt you. I don't want to have to kill you and your brothers also. Because if you don't leave right know, they are going to have to come after me for hurting you and I will have to kill them too."

I turned to leave. I knew that he was serious, and I was scared. As I turned to leave the room, he jumped me from behind. He was trying to throw me down to the floor. I tried to stay on my feet and push him off of me. I felt something pop in my knee and down I went. He was all over me hitting and kicking me. I got to my feet somehow and ran into the living room. I was so scared; he was raging and closing in on me. I screamed and the kids woke up and Alana ran into the living room. "Stop, Daddy! Leave her alone!!!" my son yelled from down the hallway.

"Get back in the bedroom," Darnell yelled at Alana. She ran. As he turned to see if she had left the room, he loosened his grip on me. I ran to the phone and dialed 911, that's all the time I had before he ran over to me and grabbed the phone out of my hands and hung up. I knew that all I had to do was to dial 911 and hang up and the police could trace my call. I had only learned this fact a few days earlier through a conversation with a friend of mine at work. Thank God for that conversation or I don't know what would have happened. He continued to beat me and push me around. I could hardly get away from him because my leg was starting to hurt bad. The phone rang and I ran to it and picked up the receiver. "Did anyone call 911 from this phone?"

"Yes, yes" was all I had time to say before he jerked the phone out of my hand and threw it. He starting throwing Christmas decorations all around the room. He picked up one of those thick round candles I had sitting on the bookcase and threw it at me. I ducked and it hit the wall with such force that the impact put a hole in the wall. He grabbed me and threw me on the sofa that was close to the front door. I sat up trying to get away from him but he had me cornered. He started slapping me repeatedly on the left side of my head, right at my temple. Each time he slapped me, he told me about how I would feel when he told my children about how I had been whoring around on him. He just kept slapping me and cursing me, when all of a sudden, there was a knock at the door.

It seemed as if he was in a trance all the time he was slapping me. When he heard the knock at the door, he straightened up. He reached over and opened the door; thank God there was a policeman there.

"Is everything all right here?" he asked. Darnell backed away from the door and walked across the room to sit in a chair. I let the policeman in and told him that my husband had attacked me.

"Is that true, sir?" the policeman asked.

All Darnell could say was "I can't believe you called the police. I can't believe you did this."

What did he expect me to do, allow him to beat me to a pulp, or maybe even kill me? "Would you like to press charges, miss?" the policeman asked me. I really wanted to, but my mind started ticking, whirling thoughts around about his standing in the community and him perhaps losing his job and a possible lose of income.

"No, just take him away tonight," I told the officer. Darnell was still very disturbed, very agitated and I do believe he still wanted to do me harm. The officer took him outside. I could hear him ranting and raving and going on and on about what I had done wrong, about my affair. The policeman left a form with me to show Darnell just in case he decided to raise a hand to me again. All I had to do was to turn him in and he would go to jail. He offered to have someone take me to the hospital, because my leg was obviously injured. I declined; all I wanted to do was to have him take Darnell away.

After they left, I fell apart. Alana and Stephen came running in and we all hugged each other very tightly. We all were badly shaken and the kids asked if they could sleep with me. They helped me pick things up that had been knocked over and I got a bag of frozen vegetables out of the freezer to put on my knee. All three of us climbed into bed together and tried to sleep. Stephen said that he never wanted to see his father again and he hoped that he never came back. Alana was sucking her thumb like crazy. She was a thumb sucker and when she got upset, she really went to town on that thumb. About two hours later, the phone rang and I knew who it was.

I picked up the receiver, "Hello," I said. No answer—I knew it was Darnell. "I know that this is you. I don't understand what drove you to do such a thing. I don't care what it was I did in the past, I did not deserve the beating you gave me tonight. No one does. My leg is hurt and I can hardly walk. I believe I will have to go to the hospital if it's not better by morning. All these years that I have been with you, and you know they have been hard years. Does that not tell you something; does that not tell you that I have some feelings for you? What do you want from me? All I can do is say that I'm sorry for what I did, but that was well over a year ago. If I didn't want to be with you, I would have left a long time ago. Why do you think I've stayed with you all these years? It can't be for the money because you've never had any. I either love you or I'm just a fool." I told him it was because I loved him all the while thinking that I was just a fool. Why was I staying with this man? I needed to find out, needed to find out what made me tick and why I put up with so much stuff from him. He never uttered one word on the other end; after I had my say I just hung up.

The next morning, my knee was swollen, I couldn't bend it and I knew I had to drive to Camille's school to pick her up for the holidays; some holiday this would be. I called my sister Lizzie and told her what happened; I asked her if she would go to pick Camille up for me. But she was afraid to go too far out of town because she was expecting her baby any day. I asked her if she would at least come and take me to the emergency room.

We were sitting in the emergency room within the hour. I stayed there all morning getting X-rays and being examined. I made up a lie about injuring myself while exercising. This is what I told everybody at work also. When I left the hospital, my left leg was in a removable cast from my ankle up to my thigh. We went home and I took Darnell's Christmas present out from under the tree—it was a CD player—and unwrapped it and had my sister take it back to the store to get a refund. With that money, I brought a cane to help me walk and paid for prescriptions for pain and swelling. The rest, I pocketed. I hugged my sister and thanked her. Then the kids and I got in my car; I propped my leg up on my purse on the floor of the car and drove the two hours to Camille's school to pick her up.

To say that we had a Merry Christmas was a lie. By Christmas, Darnell had eased his way back into the house. He stayed out of sight for days. He holed up in Stephen's room for a few days and would enter and leave the house by the bedroom window. He had left letter of apology number one thousand telling me how awful he felt when he saw me walking around with a cane and how it crippled his mind to see how much he had hurt me. I didn't want to hear it; I had come to the conclusion that this man was not all there in the mental department. We got through Christmas as best as we could; he spent most of the time gone, which was a blessing. He got me an exercise bike for Christmas of all things, like I could use it. I had made up in my mind that I was going to make a change in my life. This is something that is easier said than done, especially if you have lived one way for most of your life.

It took my leg about three months to heal. After that, I started working out again and using that bike Darnell had gotten me for Christmas. Darnell and I hardly saw each other. I had gotten addicted to working out, but it seemed no matter how hard I tried to lose weight, it would not come off. It was very frustrating; I was eating all the right foods and working out every day. I just couldn't understand why I couldn't lose weight.

Chapter 19

One day, at work my coworker went to her OB/GYN; we just happened to have the same doctor. She asked me when was the last time I had been; it had been well over two years. She convinced me to go; I had been having some trouble with my bladder, and I couldn't hold my water too good. After his examination, he told me that he had discovered that I had a tumor. After further examinations and questions, it was determined that I would need a hysterectomy and also I had to have my bladder tacked up. It seemed that the tumor was quite large and had caused my bladder to fall. The doctor watched me for months until he determined that I could not go on any further without having this operation. My condition had started affecting my kidneys. We decided that I would go in the hospital that summer.

By that summer, my sister and her husband and new baby girl (their daughter was born on Christmas Day) had moved to Charlotte, North Carolina. We had our family reunion in Charlotte that summer and I was scheduled to go in the hospital a couple of days after the reunion. Darnell did not attend the event; he never attended too many of our family reunions. I would ask him to come, but he would always decline, which I knew he would. By that time, I had come to the conclusion that he was a social outcast anyway.

I went in to the hospital and had my surgery and everything was a success. My mom and my oldest sister Janie stayed at my house to assist me along with my daughter Camille. I had plenty of help those first few weeks after I got home. As I started recovering, I noticed that

I had lost a lot of weight. By the time I went back to work, I had lost at least thirty pounds and was looking good. This gave me all the encouragement to continue my diet and my exercising. I started feeling really good about how I looked, but something was still bothering me. I was almost forty years old by then and I started looking at my life and really wondering why it was the way it was.

I started reading a book I had brought years ago when I lived in Atlanta. *Women Who Love Too Much*; the subtitle is *when you keep hoping he will change*. I picked up that book and started reading it. So many symptoms of these women hit home for me. A lot of these types of women, who sounded more and more like me, had grown up in a home where alcohol was abused. I started wondering about myself. I felt as if I had become an alcoholic, that I needed to go to AA. But I couldn't bring myself to do that; I couldn't admit that I had a drinking problem, which I felt I did. I picked up the phone one day and called a hotline not for AA, but for Al-Anon. The symptoms given to me over the phone made me slam the receiver down. I was in tears; every symptom given sounded just like me. Somehow, I found the courage to pick the phone back up and make an inquiry about meetings for Al-Anon. I could admit that I was an adult child of an alcoholic parent, but not that I was an alcoholic.

My first meeting was very enlightening; I met people there that had the same or similar experiences that I had growing up. Some of these people had the same characteristics that I had also. Like always wanting to control situations, trying to make everyone around them happy, trying not to make waves. Each meeting that I attended left me drained and also brought back a lot of memories, emotional memories that I had buried or learned to bury in order to not feel so much pain. These meetings sent me to a place that I had not been before, a place deep within myself. I purchased a book that I carried around with me everywhere I went; the book is called *The Courage to Change*; this was Al-Anon's answer to *One Day at a Time*, the book for alcoholics. This book became my Bible; I would read it every day. I also learned the true meaning of the Serenity Prayer. I never understood those words before; I used to see that prayer from time to time, but I could not comprehend it. This prayer became a powerful prayer for me and it saw me through a lot of hard times to come. I started understanding what "acceptance" meant, what "the courage to change things" meant, and "wisdom to know the difference" meant. This prayer, along with my book *Women Who Love Too Much* took on new meaning for me. In the past, when I read that book, I took the cover off so that Darnell could not read the subtitle *when you keep hoping he will change*; this time I didn't do that. I decided not to try to control the situation that I knew would arise. He didn't understand what the book meant and I didn't waste my time explaining it to him.

"If you want to know what it means, then read it," I told him when he read the title and, of course, misunderstood what it meant. My whole outlook on life began to change and I started doing things for me, started learning how to love me, just a little at first. I started exploring who I was and what I was all about, me—not the wife or mother, but Carol the woman.

I started facing a lot of things about myself that I didn't like. For example, the fact that I had been living a lie for eighteen years, married to a man that I tried to be "in love" with and never succeeded. I really and truly did not want to be with him any longer, didn't want to sleep with him; I didn't want to have sex with him. The bottom line, I didn't want to lie to myself anymore, didn't want to sell myself short anymore and I truly didn't want to take another drink just to be with him in bed anymore. The night I discovered this was when he had a day off from work. We were sitting in the den; I knew he wanted to make love. God knows I didn't, I kept hoping he would go to sleep, but instead, he invited me back into the bedroom.

"Don't you want to have a few drinks first?" I asked him.

"No, all I want is you," he said moving back into the bedroom.

"I'll be right there," I told him all the time reaching for the refrigerator door. I took a beer out and chugged it, then went to the bedroom. I climbed into bed with him, and I realized that I didn't have a buzz on.

"Just a minute, Darnell, I need to go to the bathroom," I lied. I went straight for the kitchen and tried to chug another beer. It wouldn't go down and I just stood there looking at the can. It was then that I realized that this was it, I couldn't go on any longer pretending, and it had to stop. I felt as if I was killing myself by drinking so much just to stay where I didn't want to be. I emptied the beer down the drain; I still didn't have the courage to refuse Darnell. I went back into the bedroom and we made love. Or he made love to me, I just endured it for the last time.

The next morning, I sat at my dinner table in the den and wrote him a letter. I felt like a coward, but this was the only way I could tell him what I was about to tell him. I tried to explain myself to him, tried to let him know "the me" that I finally had to face. I knew he wouldn't be able to comprehend what I was saying. I told him that I was sorry, but I couldn't love him the way he wanted me to. I still didn't have the nerve to tell him that I didn't love him anymore, but that letter was the first step to my freedom from the false life that I was living. The letter was two pages long; I finished it and put it in an envelope, laid it on the dining room table and left the house. I got in the car and turned the ignition on, then turned it off. Got out of my car, went back into the house and over to the table. I picked the letter up and stared at it, and then I put it back on the table and ran out of the house. I started the car, backed it out of the driveway and drove off. As I got further and further away from the house, I felt these wings sprout in my back and I felt wonderful. I did it, I finally did it, I told the truth and whatever will be, will be.

I knew that I would be getting a call from him at work later that day and I did. He was confused, wasn't sure what I meant; I'm sure he knew but was in denial. He was convinced that I was confused because of the Al-Anon meetings that I had been attending and that I didn't know what I was saying. He basically brushed the letter off as if it meant nothing. I guess I will have to tell it to his face and not beat around the bush. I had to pick the right time.

It was almost Christmas around this same time, so I decided to leave things until after the holidays. My daughter Camille came home for the holidays. I had expected her to stay for a couple of weeks, but she left a few days after Christmas to be with her boyfriend's family. I thought she would be going back to school soon after her visit with his family. Instead, she came back to the house for a few more days. I was in my bedroom when she came in; I could always tell when something was on her mind.

"Mom, I need to ask you something." The look on her face was one of concern.

"What is it, Camille?"

"Mom, I need to know more about my real father, David. I need to know about your relationship."

Well, I really wasn't expecting that question from her. I had always told her about him and our relationship, I had always told her how we felt about each other back then. What I didn't tell her or anybody else was that I was still in love with him. That I never stopped loving him and that I still dreamed about him all the time; and that in my dreams, we were always looking for each other, but would seem to always just miss each other. When I dreamed of him, I would wake up and it was as if he was inside of me; I carried him around with me for days. I could feel his presence all around me wherever I went. Then, after a few days, the feeling would go away, I would force myself to bury my feelings and not think about him. I often wondered where he was and how he was doing. I felt that he wasn't doing too well; all I heard about him when I would go home for a visit was that he was in jail or that he was on drugs. I never told Camille about that part of him, only about our love that we shared years ago. Now, here she is all grown up and wondering and she had every right to wonder, but why now at this time in my life?

Chapter 20

"Mom, do you know where he is? I want to try to find him and just try to meet him. Will you help me?"

I tried to stay calm and collected. "I know that his mother lives just a few blocks from Mom. I still have an old phone book from back home. We can look her address up and, if you want to write him there, I'm sure she can get the letter to him," I told her. She really didn't know what she was asking of me, but I couldn't turn her down: she had a right to know her real father. So I gave her the address and when she went back to school, she wrote him a letter.

After she left, I started questioning myself about the past, started getting all these realizations. I realized that I had deprived my daughter of her birthright, of an entire family that lived in the same town that she did when she was a small child. I remember being in the same church building with David's mother one evening. I had Camille with me and I looked up and saw her with two of her other grandchildren. The urge to take Camille over to meet her was so strong that it almost knocked me out of the pew. But I didn't do it; I didn't know how she would respond to Camille and me. I didn't want to be rejected by her, didn't want my child to be rejected either, so I left it alone.

I remember seeing David on a corner one day. He asked if he could see his daughter, and I told him "no," that I didn't want to confuse her, she was so young. David had seven brothers and one sister, which meant that Camille had a host of kin people all around her for years and she didn't even know them. She even went to the same elementary school with her older half-sister and I never told her about it. How could I have done that to my own child? This realization hit me like a ton of bricks; I went around for weeks beating myself up, trying to rationalize my actions. I started crying all the time, still attending my Al-Anon meetings twice a week; this was the only time I felt that all would be well. For weeks I went around crying and beating myself up about all the mistakes I had made all my life. My marriage, Camille, and I was still facing a lot of facts about my childhood, living with my alcoholic father and all the things I experienced with that life. I was on edge all the time, couldn't sleep or eat. This did do wonders for my figure, however.

Camille called me at work one day; she told me that she had gotten a letter from David. My heart was pounding so hard I could hardly breathe. I had been wondering if he had gotten her letter and if he did, if he would answer it.

"Mom, it's the most beautiful letter I have ever read!"

"Really, Camille? Would you mind reading it to me?" I really wanted to know how he was doing and also if he asked about me.

She was right; it was a very beautiful letter. He told her that he was living in Louisville, Kentucky, and that he was saved and deeply involved in the church and he wanted to know if she was saved also. That he loved her very much and that he had never gone one day without praying for her and wondering where she was. He said that he knew that she was all right because he knew that I would be a good mother. He asked about me and if I was doing all right. The letter went on and on. He told her that he would call her soon. I was so flabbergasted and so thankful that he was doing just fine. Now, I had to deal with my feelings for him; they started unearthing themselves from the grave I had buried them in deep within my heart years ago.

If I wasn't crazy before, well I sure was now. I spent most of my days just existing, always in deep thought about everything that seemed to be going on at the same time. I have heard that age forty starts a new and exciting time in a female's life. I really wasn't expecting that kind of excitement!

Then, the day came; I guess fate just stepped in. I was at home just yelling at Alana about something; Darnell came out of the bedroom, which was where he practically lived.

"What is wrong with you? Why are you yelling like that? Come back to the bedroom, we have to talk." I followed him back to the bedroom, he sat upon the bed, and I sat on the floor next to the bedroom door.

"What's going on with you? I know that you are going through a lot but is it that bad? What is it? Is living with me so bad that you seem to have just lost your mind?" he asked.

My mind went back to one of my Al-Anon meetings; more than one woman had confessed that they had married men that they didn't love. I decided that I was not going any further with my lie, I was going to answer him.

"Darnell, I tried to tell you weeks ago in that letter how I was feeling. Do you remember what I said?"

"What is it, Carol? Do you love me at all?"

Now was the time. I looked at him sitting on the bed, I knew I had to tell him. "No, I don't love you, not like you want me to. I love you because we have been together for a very long time. But I am not in love with you."

He looked at me as if his world was coming to an end. "Did you ever love me?" His voice was trembling and he had tears in his eyes. I had started crying also.

"Darnell, I learned to love you, but down through the years—the way you are, you are a very hard man to love. What feeling I had for you died a long time ago. I'm sorry but I can't go on living this lie any longer." He fell back on the bed as if someone had shot him. I couldn't stay in that room any longer; I went into the den and got the kids and we went out for a long drive.

When we returned, the house was silent. I went back to the bedroom looking for Darnell but he wasn't there. Then I heard him behind me; I turned to face him not knowing what to expect. He took my hands and looked me straight in the eyes.

"Carol, I love you very much and I don't want to lose you. I'm telling you now that I am going to fight to keep you."

I didn't know what to say to that. I knew that eventually, I would have to hit him in between the eyes with the fact that I wanted a divorce. How he had intended to fight for me, I didn't quite know. It was almost time for him to go to work; I was thankful for that. I was also waiting for a major explosion from him, but it never came. What came were days and nights of him tuning in to any and every religious program on TV. I realized that he was searching for some answers and some peace. I even got a strange charge on the phone bill one month from the physic hotline. When I saw that bill, I immediately called my son in the den and ask him about it. "It wasn't me. Maybe Alana did it." She denied making the call, which left only one person, Darnell.

"What were you trying to find out? Did they tell you what you wanted to hear?" I asked him. He wouldn't answer me, just looked off into the distance. I couldn't stand the way we were living, under the same roof and our marriage being over as far as I was concerned. The strain was too hard to bare when we were both at the house together; there were constant question and answer periods.

"Do you want a divorce?" he asked me one day.

"Yes, I want a divorce," I told him.

"I can't believe you really want a divorce, that you really don't love me, you're just confused."

"No, I'm not confused; I see everything very clearly for the first time in my life. I don't want to be married to you any longer." He stared at me with deep penetrating eyes.

"Can you tell me if this time next year that you will want to be with me again?"

"What kind of question is that? I don't know what I will be doing in the next minute, let alone this time next year?"

Then, finally one day, he asked me to give him a few months and he would be out of the house. I said all right, but I really didn't believe him. So I started saving money; I knew that I would have to be the one to make the move, not him. I did wish that he would go, but that would have been too easy.

I spent each day at work receiving calls from him trying to convince me that I was committing a sin by leaving him. That divorce was wrong in the eyes of the Lord; some days his calls bordered on harassment. Meanwhile, I was still thinking about David a lot. I had told a couple of my coworkers about him and all of the feelings I was having.

We had gone out to lunch one day and when we got back, one of the girls called the front desk to retrieve our messages. She started writing down our calls and as she wrote them she was repeating what she was writing. "Yeah, okay. David Houser for Carol."

When I heard that name, I thought I was going to faint, I jumped up and ran out of the office and into the bathroom down the hall. My heart was pounding and I had tears in my eyes. No, no, this cannot be happening; it couldn't be him that called. It had been so long; so much time had passed, a whole lifetime. Camille had given him my number at work; he said that he had wanted to call me just to talk but I never thought that he would actually call. Now, I was faced with the prospect of talking to him after all this time. What would he sound like, what would we say to each other, did he still have feelings for me like I had for him? So much emotion was flooding my heart, my mind; it took a long time before I could come out of that bathroom stall. When I did, I walked back into my office with everyone looking at me like I was crazy, which was how I felt.

"That name, that is Camille's real father—oh my God, Carol, that was him. Do you think he will call back?" my coworkers started quizzing me.

"I don't know. Maybe I will call him back—I don't know—maybe I should just wait—no, I'll call him." I was a nervous wreck; I picked up the phone, knowing that this call would change my life forever.

I dialed the number that was left with the receptionist with trembling fingers. A female picked up the phone. "Hello." I wondered who she was.

"May I speak to David please?"

"I'm sorry but he is asleep right now," the female voice said on the other end. Should I leave a message or just hang up? I decided to leave a message.

"Would you tell him that Carol returned his call please?"

"Carol, oh wait just a minute I will wake him up," the voice on the other side of the phone said. I almost hung the phone up, so nervous, it seemed like I had been waiting all my life to talk to him just one more time. Now, after over eighteen years, the time had finally come around, I heard him pick the receiver up

"Hello, Carol" were his first words.

"Hello, David. How are you?"

Chapter 21

"I married the wrong woman, all those years ago; it should have been you, not her. I have never stopped loving you; there was never a day that went by that I have not thought about you and our daughter."

I couldn't believe what I was hearing from this man, that he still loved me.

"David, I still love you too. I have never stopped loving you, never."

We started pouring our hearts out to one another. We talked about that night on the street when he stood between his fiancée and me. We talked about how he thought that he had lost his daughter to another man. How he spent the last eighteen years thinking, through some miscommunication, that Darnell had adopted his child. How he had turned to drugs to forget the pain. So many misunderstandings down through the years; so much time wasted on hearsay. He told me how he punished himself every day because he knew that he had given up the woman that he truly loved and his daughter.

We poured our hearts out to each other that day, but at the end of our conversation, decided that we should not do anything about our feelings. He respected the fact that I was married even though I was trying to get a divorce. He didn't want to come between Darnell and me in case we decided to get back together. He was just coming out of a bad relationship himself that left him with a three-year-old son to raise; his situation wasn't too good. Apparently he had just relocated to Kentucky with his son and was staying with his sister until he could get back on his feet. He had taken his son with him to West Virginia to bury one of his brothers. Apparently, his life in Ohio where he had been living was not what he wanted for himself or his son. Once his brother was buried, he decided not to return to his home or his sons' mother. He left his home, clothes, his job and his woman behind in Ohio and continued on to Kentucky to start a new life. It seemed as if the two of us were going through a lot of changes.

I really wanted to try to have some sort of relationship with him, but he felt it was best if we just put some closure on what we had. That we acknowledged that we would always be in love with each other, but our lives were just a little too complicated right now. We needed to think with our heads instead of our hearts. I knew what he was saying was right, but my heart was overruling my head at the moment. All I knew was that I had found my true love once again and that I was starved for that love. I needed the type of love I knew he was capable of giving, not just physically, but spiritually and emotionally; it seemed so close yet so far. I didn't want to end the conversation for I knew that I might not hear from him again. He told me that he didn't want to say goodbye but it would be best for us to hang up. I could hear and feel the emotion in his voice; I know that we both had shed some tears during that long conversation.

Finally, we said goodbye and when I hung the phone up my heart dropped; I burst into tears. I thought about how unfair the world can be sometimes and wondered why; after what seemed like a lifetime had passed my heart had started beating again and for what? A love that once was when I was too young to appreciate it and now that I'm old enough to take that love and hold it close to my heart, it may never be. I couldn't function for the rest of the day; all I did was go over that phone call and try to figure out how to bury my love for that man again. I knew that this would be the only way for me to go on. I had to find that place that I had put David all those years ago and place him back in there, but I didn't have the strength to find that grave. I knew it was time to deal with this part of my life just like it was time for me to deal with everything else that was coming up and slapping me right in the face.

It seemed as if all the bad decisions that I had ever made in the past were coming back to haunt me now. The decision to marry a man that I really didn't love; and to keep my child from her birth father and his family. All these I made when I was a mere child; now it seemed as if everything was coming full circle. When would that circle close?

After about a week had passed and I had not gotten any better, all I could think about was David. I called a very good friend of mine; I felt as if I was dying inside and this is what I told her. She told me to pick up the phone and call that man; it would make me feel better if I talked to him, she said. Well, that was all I needed to hear from her. I hung the phone up and after about an hour, I finally dialed his number. His sister answered the phone, I asked for him and then I heard his voice again.

"I'm sorry, I know you wanted to end things, but I just had to talk to you."

"Hello, Carol. I'm so glad you called because I needed to talk to you also." He didn't have my home phone but I had his. I started feeling so much better; talking to him I told him a lot about my marriage and my children and he told me about his life. That he had only stayed married to Tonya for about five or six years and that he had never remarried. That he had a lot of relationships, but through them all there was always me.

"I love you, Carol, and always will. I always told my family how special you was to me. They all know about you and Camille and how much I love both of you. Every woman I have had a relationship with, I have always told them about you and our child. About my soul mate, somewhere out there and now we have found each other again."

I was so happy; I didn't know what to do. We decided that there was no way we could stay away from each other. We really didn't know how things were going to work out, but that we would keep in touch somehow. I felt as if I had my true love back now and that I would just have to be patient and one day, we would be together.

I started taking very long walks in the evenings after work, just to clear my head. On the days that Darnell was off work, my walks were extra long. I really didn't want to be in the same house with him at all. Everybody was just miserable under that roof; sometimes Alana would go with me. We would walk and talk about all sorts of things, but the main thing was, when would her daddy be leaving. She really wanted him to go; she told me that she felt fine when he wasn't around. But when he came home the house would get *"dark"*; I knew exactly what she meant; the house would get dark. I told her to be patient, that we might have to move ourselves because I really didn't think he was going to leave.

Camille and I started having lots of conversations about David and Darnell. She was in a situation, not knowing how to handle having two fathers. She wanted Darnell to know that she loved him and always would and that just because she had found her birth father, that fact didn't change her feelings for him. I had told Darnell about Camille finding David and I knew he felt threatened by this fact. I told him about Camille's position, that she felt stuck between her two fathers. She really wanted to talk to Darnell about the situation, but she didn't know how to approach him. I asked him to please make the first move to make it easier for her. He didn't understand what I meant.

"She knows where I am, she needs to come to me," was his reply.

"Even though she is in college, she is still a child, especially in a case such as this. You, however are an adult, you should be old enough to help her out. Why don't you invite her to lunch so the two of you can talk about this, father to daughter?"

He agreed to do it, but against his own judgment. The lunch went fine; they both talked about the situation and felt better after that.

"Mom, Dad has some weird ideas about you. I can't believe, after all these years that you two have been together, he really does not know you at all," Camille told me after the lunch date. This was something I had realized years before; he didn't know me at all. It seems like he was always off the mark as far as really knowing who I was deep inside.

I was very careful not to let him know that I had been talking to David on a regular basis. I was still afraid that he would go off at any time. He told me that he knows that his violent temper in the past is the cause of me leaving him. That he would not be that way any longer. I really was not interested in hearing that; all I wanted was for him to leave. He asked me to give him four months, but it didn't seem as if he was making any effort to find a new place to live.

Easter was coming up and the kids and I had planned to travel to West Virginia to spend some time with my mother. This was also the time that David had planned to come home also to see his daughter and myself. Camille did not know, although I'm sure she suspected that David and I were back together again. We had a system for communicating. He would call me on the nights that David was not at home or he would call me at work during the day whenever he was off work and I had purchased a post office box for the countless letters and cards he was sending. Sometimes I would get two letters at once. Our love was in full blossom; all we needed was to see and touch each other.

The two of us had been connected again as we had when we were young but with so much more feeling and appreciation for what we had. Even though we had not seen each other in over eighteen years, we knew that we loved one another very much. Loved each other the way some people dream about but never experience. I would pray to God, thanking him for allowing me to be able to experience such a deep love and if it happens that we never got to be together the way we wanted, then that was alright. Like Marvin Gaye said, "How many eyes have seen their dreams, how many arms have felt their dreams, how many hearts have felt their world stand still. Millions never will they never will." But we had felt that and I was so grateful to God for showing me the difference between just loving someone and being in love with someone. There is such a broad difference between the two. All these feelings I had without even being with this man; I had been with the boy but now he was a man and I was a woman. Even though we had not been intimate with each other as adults, I knew how true love felt with him. Soon we would be together in each other's arms and we couldn't wait. He also couldn't wait to see his daughter whom he had dreamed about for so many years.

"Baby, what will I say to her, how should I act?" he would ask me.

"Act like the beautiful man that you are and everything will be just fine," I told him. He would call me at work a lot; sometimes I would not be at my desk and he would leave me such beautiful messages.

"Where are you? I need to hear your voice today. I need to tell you that I love you and I miss you and I want you, I can't wait to touch you once again." Those kinds of messages would just make me melt. I was almost like a schoolgirl again; I would save his messages and play them over and over just to hear his voice. This man is like no other that I have ever known, in touch with himself and his feelings, not afraid to love or to give love, a very tender and gentle person. I could say anything to him, tell him my deepest secrets, all my hopes and dreams and he would accept them because they were a part of me. He loved my other two children even though he had never met them; "Because they are a part of you," is what he told me.

The time came for us to travel to West Virginia. My sister Lizzie came up from Charlotte where she now lived; she had two children by this time, a boy and a girl. We drove up in her car and we had such a lovely trip. Camille and I were both nervous wrecks anticipating our meeting with David. My sister was happy for me, but also reminded me that I was committing a sin since I was still married to someone else even though I was trying to get out of that situation. But she still supported me and wanted me to be happy.

The plan was for David and I to see each other that very night and the next day, he would come over to take Camille out to lunch and then to his mother's house to meet some of her other family. When we got to Mom's house, there was a bouquet of Easter flowers waiting for Camille from David. She was very impressed by that, but I could tell that she had a lot of mixed emotions about seeing him for the first time in her life. I was a nervous wreck all that day after we arrived home waiting for him to call to say where we would meet that evening. We all busied ourselves getting prepared for the Easter holiday and just sitting around visiting each other.

Chapter 22

The evening wore on slowly for me. Every time the phone rang, I jumped to answer it; finally around nine he called. I was to drive the two blocks to his mother's house to pick him up and then we would go to a motel to be alone. I was running around the house trying to get ready and my sister was running around behind me dressing me. It was as if we were two teenagers getting ready for a date. I was nervous about what my mother would say; I'm sure she knew that I was going to meet David. I was ready to walk through the house and out the door; Mom was sitting in the living room watching TV.

"What will I tell her, Lizzie?"

"How old are you, forty or fourteen? Just walk out the door and say 'I'll see you later, Mom,'" she told me.

"Yeah, you're right, I'll just walk out the front door." On my way past Mom I told her that I was going out. I was getting ready for her to say something to me like "Where do you think you are going?"

But all she said was "Fix your tag on your blouse; it's out in the back."

That was easy, I thought, so I fixed my tag and before I knew it, I was driving up to David's mother's house. I didn't know if I should park or blow the horn or what. Just as I was deciding to park, I looked up on the front porch and saw him come out of the house. He had the same nice body that he had in high school, only filled out like a man. My heart was pounding; what would he think of me after all these years? He got into the car and we stared at each other for a long time.

"You look great," he told me while reaching over to give me a small kiss.

"You look good too, David."

"Park the car and let's go in so you can meet my mother," he told me. I was so nervous that I could hardly back up to park the car correctly. We both got out of the car and joined hands and walked into his mother's house. There I met her and his sister Tricia, her daughter Ava and his son Davie. They all hugged me when we met; I got such a warm welcome from them all, and this made me feel good inside. We all sat around for just a short time talking and then the two of us left.

We stopped by the corner store to get some sodas. He asked me if I wanted some wine to drink. I knew that he was testing me; I had stopped drinking months before after I joined Al-Anon, I had no need to drink anymore. My whole outlook on life had changed, especially since I had gotten back with David. After he got back into the car, he told me that he was testing me; I told him that I knew that.

We never had an awkward moment from the time he got into my car like some people would after a long absence. It was as if we had never left each other, as if we just picked up from where we left off all those years before. During the drive to the motel we couldn't keep our hands off of each other. Not in a groping sexual way, but just touching each other with very gentle caresses. Once the door closed behind us in the motel room, we embraced each other for a long, long time. Nothing was said, we just stood in the middle of the room in an embrace so close that you couldn't tell where one of us began and the other one ended. We kissed and kissed each other, caressed each other's arms, chest, and face, looked deeply into each other's eyes for a very long time. It was as if we both could not believe that we were standing in front of each other. Finally, he took me by the shoulders and sat me down on one bed and he sat on the other bed.

"Let's talk; I have to sit across from you for now, otherwise we will never get any conversation in."

The conversation didn't last too long. Before we knew it, we were in each other's arms making love to one another over and over again. This was like nothing I had ever experienced, I was actually making love to someone that I wanted, needed to be with, and he was making love to me. He was a gentle and considerate lover, making sure that I was being satisfied. The love we made was a sweet love, it felt so pure and natural like this was supposed to be. I never wanted to leave that room and go back to the real world. After we finished making love, we just lay in the bed and talked to each other very gently all the time caressing each other.

"You know you just committed adultery don't you?" he asked me all the time smiling.

"No, I don't feel as if I have, not with you, I feel as if I belong with you, like I'm a part of you."

He took me in his arms and kissed me deeply. I didn't feel like I was doing anything wrong, I just felt so complete with him and so much in love. We just talked and smiled and touched each other while lying on the bed facing one another. What a beautiful night we had together, but we had to leave soon; we had not planned to be out all night long. After all, the next day would be a big day for David and Camille.

That next day turned out to be a day full of wonder in more ways than one. At first we all wondered when David was coming to pick Camille up for lunch. He was supposed to arrive at noon, but he didn't show up until around 1:00. Then we wondered how everything was going for them during their first meeting over lunch. I went through that entire day glowing after the night the two of us had together. I was completely and totally in love, in another world—gone. I couldn't do anything right that day. I made a bowl of potato salad for Easter dinner and forgot to put half of the ingredients in it. My mom gave me one of those "this poor pitiful child" looks and said, "You just cannot do anything right today. can you? Just got David Houser on the brain, don't you?"

I gave her, I am sure a really stupid smile; "Yeah" was all I could say back to her. She just shook her head and watched me while I put the rest of the ingredients into the potato salad.

Camille and David had been gone for quite some time. I was anxious to see how things went between the two of them. I went over in my mind the events from just a few hours ago. I believe that everyone in that household was nervous and excited. My brother James just happened to be visiting for the holiday also; he and David used to hang together when we were all young. As the time approached for David's arrival, we all got busy. Mom and Camille were downstairs in the kitchen talking and working; Lizzie, James, and I went upstairs to look at some home videos that he had taken of his family. We were all awaiting the arrival of Camille's father and our old friend (my lover) to arrive. Finally, I heard my mother call out to Camille, "Here he comes."

We all piled down the stairs to meet him; he had his son little Davie with him. He was welcomed with opened arms; it was a reunion of old friends and family, a very special moment. He hugged and kissed Lizzie and my mom and was very surprised and happy to see my brother James. Then he turned to see Camille. "Is this my daughter?" was all he could get out.

He reached out to her and hugged her tightly; she gave him a very tentative hug back, not quite knowing how to respond. We all sat around and talked for a while and then, they were out the door and walking down the sidewalk to his car. He took hold of her hand gently and never let it go all the time that they walked to the car.

When she finally came back, of course she was quizzed about the events of the afternoon. After lunch, he took her by his mother's house so she could meet her and she was greeted by a host of kin people. She was shown loads of pictures of, as she said, people that she probably would never meet nor remember.

This was said with a tinge of animosity in her voice. I sensed this tone and tried to analyze the reason behind it. Feelings of guilt crept into my mind for not allowing her to ever meet those people she was referring to.

I talked to my mother about these feelings and she said, "They knew where Camille was all those years she was living here. They could have just as easily approached her themselves."

She was right, but I still felt guilty and very responsible for the turmoil that my daughter was apparently going through. Later that day, my best friend since junior high, Alice, came down to visit me. We talked for a very long time about all the events in my life that had led up to this moment. "I knew you didn't love Darnell. I don't know why you married him."

"Why didn't you try to stop me?" I asked her.

"Would you have listened to me back then?" she asked.

"Probably not." She was right about that. All I wanted to do was to get married, even though deep down inside I knew that I shouldn't, but I did anyway.

Alice spent the rest of the day with my family; we all sat around and talked about our adventures when we were young. Later on, David came back by with his son and we all sat in the living room visiting. The room was full of people all talking and laughing. David and I sat across the room from each other; even though we were far away from one another, we could feel each other. It was like a pull or some invisible force that we could feel between the two of us, a connection. We had planned to see each other later on that night and I could hardly wait until we were alone again.

Before David and little Davie left Mom's house, his older son and his niece stopped by to meet Camille. I could not imagine what she was feeling; I'm sure very overwhelmed by it all. It seemed as if we all were forcing her new family down her throat, trying to make up for all of those lost years. I expected her to be elated and much more receptive to everything than it seemed that she was. I tried to read her, but I couldn't; I guess I was too caught up in my own fantasy to see that she was very overwhelmed. I found myself trying to sell David to her and her boyfriend who had come along with Camille on the trip. He and Camille rode up in a separate car than Lizzie and I. "David is a nice man isn't he, Alan?" I asked him.

His answer was a very reserved "Yes, ma'am."

I kept telling Camille about his good qualities instead of allowing her to find out about them on her own. I guess I just wanted everything to be perfect for all involved overnight. I wanted all those years of absence to be wiped away in one weekend.

We met later that night. "I wanted us to go to another hotel, but I'm a little low on cash. Do you mind if we just ride around and talk?" he asked. I was so in love, I didn't care where we went as long as we could be together. We went out to the park and road around for a while then decided to park the car and walk. It was very romantic; we walked hand in hand, the night was a little chilly, but I didn't mind that at all. We sat on a park bench; I laid my head on his shoulder while he put his arm around me.

"I know you want us to be together and you want that to happen very soon," he began. "There is so much that I have to accomplish now that I am starting my life over. So many people I have to prove myself to, starting with Camille and the rest of my children." Camille was number two of his four children. He had a son and daughter by his first wife and his young son Davie. He continued, "I have to find a place to live and buy furniture for that place. I need to make sure my oldest son gets out of this town before it eats him up. He needs to leave and get away from the lifestyle he is leading before he gets in trouble."

All the time he was telling me this, I saw a huge mountain growing right in front of my eyes, a mountain of baggage from both of our past lives.

"You're not even divorced, you still live with your husband and we both live so far away from each other. We have got to calm down and think with our heads, not our hearts, and pray for patience. Do you understand what I am saying to you, Carol?"

"Yes, I hear you, and I know that as long as we have each other, we can work everything out eventually." These words I said, but did not want to accept them, but I had no choice. We decided to take things one day at a time; that's all we could do.

We spent the rest of the night driving around and talking; we ended up parking down a lonely dark road and climbed in the back seat of the car and made love. He apologized for not having enough money to take me to a nice hotel. "I really wanted to get a nice room downtown for us, but my funds ran short."

I didn't care about that; I just wanted to be near him. I still couldn't believe that I was finally with this man that I had loved all my life; I was so happy. After we left our lonely dark road, we parked in a parking lot near my mother's home and talked for hours. We talked about things that we experienced in our past, tried to catch up on being away from each other for almost two decades, not wanting the night to end, not wanting to hear the birds singing when morning started to dawn. I didn't want morning to come because I knew that would mean sometime during that dawning day, we would have to say goodbye, he would go back to Kentucky and I would be going back to North Carolina and to a life that I no longer wanted.

We planned to attend Easter service together at my home church even though we had stayed up most of the night. I slept for a few hours and got up to get ready for church. My entire family attended service and David and his son sat with us. Afterwards, we parted to have Easter dinner with our own families. I was growing sad and depressed. He promised me that he would call me before they left for Kentucky to say goodbye. Time passed and with every ring of the phone, my heart jumped hoping it was him. But he never called; surely he would not just leave without seeing me just one more time, without seeing Camille? I picked up the phone and called my friend Alice. "He hasn't called yet. Do you think he has left, Alice?" I asked her this, afraid that all I had felt that weekend was for nothing. I was afraid of being hurt, of being disappointed by this man that I loved with all my heart. Before she could answer, he pulled up, "He's here, I'll call you later, " and I hung up.

I watched as he and Michael got out of the car and came up on the porch. "You thought I wasn't coming didn't you?"

He read my feelings so good; he has always been able to do that. I wanted to fall into his arms but I controlled myself. The goodbye was brief as it was getting late and they had to get on the road. He hugged Camille and the rest of my family, I walked him onto the porch and we embraced each other and within a few minutes, he was out of sight. When we would be able to see each other again was something that we did not know. Little did I realize that the journey I was about to take would be another one of the hardest I have ever taken.

Chapter 23

The next day, we loaded the car back up and headed to North Carolina, something that I really didn't want to do. The trip down did not take long for some reason. The closer we got to home, the more withdrawn I became. I knew that I had no choice but to return to my home with Darnell being there. Once we pulled up into the driveway and unpacked the car, I could not stay in the house; I felt as if I was going to break down crying right in front of him. All I wanted to do was to be back in the arms of the man that I loved, go back to where I had been.

I left the house and went for a very long walk through the neighborhood. I walked so far that it was almost dark by the time I reached one of my neighbors' home on my return back to the house. She was in the front yard and I stopped to talk to her. I needed to talk to her; we had from time to time confided in one another when we had problems. All during my walk, I prayed and cried, tried to sort things out in my mind. Tried to convince myself to go back home, tried not to think about the wonderful weekend I had but not being able to put those memories out of my mind. Wondering how the two of us would be able to be together. Praying for God to let me have the only man I have ever really loved. Longing for my soul mate and trying to reach out to him from afar. I was an emotional wreck by the time I got to my friend's house. I believe that God knew that I needed to talk to someone and she was there for me. We talked for about an hour, when I saw Darnell's car come around the corner. I guess he got worried about me because I had been gone for so long. He passed by and just waved, turned the corner and drove home. I decided it was time for me to go home too, so I said goodbye to my friend and walked home.

The next few months were spent with Darnell and I arguing about everything; the days that he was off were miserable. He finally told me after one argument that he had decided not to leave his house.

"I know I told you that I would leave and get an apartment of my own. But I have decided that I am not going anywhere, I am not leaving my home." I can't say that I couldn't believe what I was hearing because I knew him too well.

"That's all right, I knew you wouldn't do what you said you was going to do, that's why I have been saving money to get a place of my own. It would be easier if you found a place and let me and the kids stay here in the house. Do you want to put your children out on the streets?"

"No, I'm not doing that, you are; you're the one that wants to leave, to destroy our marriage. I'll tell you another thing too: I am not going to help you out in this mess you are creating, not one bit. I'm not getting a lawyer, nor will I leave my home. You want this, you do all the work!" he shouted.

That only made me more determined to work even harder at leaving. I started looking around for an apartment big enough for the kids and myself. My mind started ticking off the pieces of furniture I would take and what I would leave behind. I started looking at my budget more carefully and planning for my move, which I calculated would take me the rest of the year to complete. I started saving every extra penny I could in order to leave when I wanted to. I decided that I would not spend my next birthday in that house. It was early summer by then and my birthday was in December.

David and I kept in touch with each other meanwhile and saw each other a few more times that year. I would travel to my mother's home and stay with her for a few days, leave the kids with her and drive the three hours to Kentucky to see him. For some reason, when we made plans to see each other, I would be the one always doing the traveling and spending a lot of money to do so. I would always have to go in

Dutch with him on our hotel rooms because he never seemed to have enough. I was so in love that it didn't matter; I felt we were a couple and it was all right to share in the expenses of our romance.

Our times together were always magical to me and his family accepted me with open arms. His sister started calling me sister-in-law and his niece started calling me auntie. I met his oldest daughter, who also lived in Kentucky, and just became one of the family. Meanwhile, my family started thinking that I had lost my mind, not spending any time with them when we had a major homecoming, meaning a lot of us would gather at my mom's house just to be with each other. Holidays like Memorial Day, Labor Day, etc., we always tried to get together as much as possible, but now I had another agenda, named David. Nobody could tell me anything about what I was doing; I had become my own person, and I liked doing what I wanted to do. This new attitude had a lot to do with my Al-Anon meetings, where I learned how to begin to do what I wanted, not what I felt people expected me to do. Therefore, I had changed according to everyone, especially my kids and of course, my husband.

The months passed by very slowly and I believe Darnell became resigned to the fact that I was really going to leave him. He clung to his newfound peace through religion as if his life depended on it. He would often come into the bedroom after I went to sleep and ask me to have prayer with him. This was something that I really didn't want to do; I had learned how to say no to him, but I didn't know how to say no to a request such as that. So I would kneel beside him and he would start praying out aloud. Asking God to help and bless the family, the kids, so on and so forth. Meanwhile, I would be praying in silence for the Lord to help me get out of my situation very quickly and to help me keep my sanity.

Around October of that year, the kids and I went apartment hunting. We looked at quite a few within the same school district so the kids would not have to change schools. We decided on a two-bedroom apartment, which was all I could afford at the time. This meant that Alana and I would have to share a bedroom and Stephen would have one to himself. Since he was almost in the twelfth grade, and college bound, Alana would get his room after he left. She was not very happy about sharing a room with her mom at all but she accepted it.

I knew I would have to tell my husband that I would be moving out in December. That was something that I was dreading, because I knew that he was still hoping that we would stay. That was something that I could not do; there was no turning back now. David and I had started talking about marriage and whether he and Little Davie would be moving down to North Carolina or if the kids and me would pack up to move to Kentucky. I felt it would be easier for him to come to us because he was still living with his sister. I would have a place for him to come to or we could save money and we could get a place big enough for all of us. I really did not want to pack all I had up to move to Kentucky when all he had could fit in his car to move to North Carolina. I didn't want to be the one in the relationship to do all the work and make all sacrifices for us to be together. I was adamant about my kids still having some roots. We had quite a few heated discussions about that issue. The decision was made to put that on the back burner until I got settled in my own place and then, we would start talking about who would relocate.

The evening I chose to tell Darnell that I would be moving was one I was not looking forward to. I really didn't know how to begin to tell him that I had set a moving date. All I kept thinking about was how he would feel once he walked back into an empty house .I kept thinking about all the years that we had been together as a family and now, he would be all alone. I beat myself up a lot about that, but I knew that I was not going to change my mind. I had to go and that was that. I still felt really bad about telling him; it was like cold reality slapping both of us in the face. He was in our bedroom, he had not been sleeping with me for months, but, after being mugged one night while on one of his walks, he needed the bed to recuperate in.

He had taken to just disappearing from the house without telling anyone; he would just leave the house. One night, I got a call from the police department telling me that my husband had been beaten pretty bad and was in the hospital. I thought it was some kind of joke, because I didn't know he had left the house and his car was still parked out front.

But sure enough, after a short search of the house and outside, I discovered that he was not home. I went to the hospital to see about him. There he was, sitting in the emergency room all bloody and beat up. He looked real bad and he was shaking all over his body.

"What happened to you? I didn't even know that you had left the house."

"I left to take a walk; I had a lot on my mind so I decided to go for a walk. I was walking down the railroad tracks and all of a sudden these two dudes jumped me from behind and just started beating me and kicking me. They were beating me all in the head with their fist; I knew they were going to kill me. I tried to get away from them, but they kept whaling away at my head. Finally, I found the strength to get away from them and run. I ran out into the street with them coming fast behind me. I ran into the street and fell. At that point, I called out to Jesus to help me, please help me. All of a sudden, as if from nowhere, these cars pulled up and the two guys ran away. I don't know what would have happened if those people hadn't come along. Now I know there is a God. I'm surprised that you are here, why are you here?" *He still doesn't know me at all,* I thought.

"Did you think that I wouldn't come to see about you? What kind of person do you think I am?"

We sat together in that emergency room for what seemed like an eternity before he was called back. It turned out that he was hurt pretty bad and would require surgery on his jaw that was broken in about four places. The rest of his body was battered and would require time to heal. I left the hospital around 4:00 a.m. and returned later that morning with the kids while he went into surgery. Even though I was leaving him, I still cared about him, didn't hate him at all. For some reason, he could not understand my actions and why I stayed with him at the hospital. He could not understand my taking care of him after he got home either.

"I still care about you, Darnell; I can't just leave you alone and not take care of you. You should know me better than that after all the years we have been together."

I came to the conclusion that he would never know me and I would no longer waste my breath trying to explain myself to him any longer.

Now, here we were, in our bedroom and I was telling him that I would be moving out on December 2.

"Thanks for telling me when you would be leaving. I will make sure that I won't be around that day. I will also make arrangements for support to be direct deposited into your bank account."

We drew up a separation agreement and had it notarized stating the amount and the arrangements for payment. He was very cooperative about that, which I appreciated.

"I told the children that they could ride the school bus over here some days if it was okay with you. I know they will miss this neighborhood and their old friends."

He was rather silent after I made that remark. "We will see about that; I'm not sure how that will work just yet," he said.

I thought that reply sounded really strange. I couldn't see what was wrong with them coming to their father's house, but I suppose he had his reasons. I didn't press him on that issue; his relationship between his kids and himself was for him to take care of. Little did I know that he was making plans of his own to move out of "his home" a month after the kids and I had already settled into our apartment. The bottom line was that he didn't want me to have the house, so instead of being honest with me about what he was about to do, he kept it to himself. I sat in that room and told him that I was leaving and would not have the need for our refrigerator, the window unit air conditioner and the clothes washer. I was leaving those for him. We decided he would keep the washer and I would take the dryer. I had no need for the other appliances as the apartment had central heat and air and a refrigerator. When he moved, he left the appliances behind in the house. When I found that out I tried to retrieve them in order to sell them for extra money. Our ex-landlords would not let me have them because Darnell had left without notice and owing them a month's rent. These appliances were in my name so I owned them, as I saw it. The air conditioner, which he said he would finish paying for, but didn't; I had to pay that off. That's not all I had to pay for, I ended up having to pay back taxes he owed from all of his freelance work in which he requested that no taxes be taken out of his pay. He would handle that at the end of the year; of course he never did. The government would take any tax money coming to me over the next few years because we had filed jointly. I guess there is always a price to pay for your freedom.

We had enough furniture to divide between the two of us for both places. The house would be a little bare, seeing how it had three bedrooms. I had left a set of bunk beds behind so the kids would have somewhere to sleep when they visited their dad. I had made arrangements for a bed for Alana and myself and a dining room table. I started packing boxes about a week before we left and tried to put them in a place where their presence would not be too disturbing to him. I could not wait to leave at that point; I didn't like seeing those boxes either just sitting around reminding everyone of what was going to happen.

Chapter 24

When the day finally came, true to his words, he was nowhere to be found. Camille and her boyfriend Alan helped us move. I went over to the apartment alone to open it up and to see if the phone had been turned on. As I walked into my new home, I burst into tears; I guess from relief that the day was finally here to start my new life and the end of the old one. Now it was time to move forward into my new future. We got moved into our new place and had all the furniture in place by that evening. I remember sitting in my easy chair by the patio doors that led onto the balcony. I looked around at my nice neat home, I looked at my two daughters and they looked at me.

"Mom, I feel like this is our home already, like we should be here." These words came from my little girl Alana.

She was so right. "I feel the same way; this feels so right." I was finally free from all those years of lies and pretense, no longer having to worry about whether I was walking or talking or looking at Darnell the right or wrong way. My heart soared with happiness that day, but boy was I tired. I decided to call David; I knew he would want to hear that all went well with the move. He wasn't home and I didn't hear from him for a couple of days.

He apologized for not calling, but was glad that we got moved in all right.

"Now I can come to see you in North Carolina. I can't wait to see you and where you live," he told me. He would call me at least twice a week and I would call him a couple of times a week also. I stopped service at the post office in order for me to start receiving letters at my home. I would go to the mailbox every day after work, anxious to hear from him, but his letters became few and far in between. I would send him cards and write to him all the time. We decided to limit our calls to once a week; our phone bills were getting out of hand. We made plans for him to come to North Carolina in the spring of that year. I had been to West Virginia and then to Kentucky the Christmas after we moved into our apartment.

On Christmas Eve, Camille and I left my mother's house early that morning and drove to Kentucky to spend the day with her father. He said it would not be a good idea for him to drive the three hours to West Virginia to see us because he wanted to spend the day at home with his son. So, after driving for five hours to West Virginia and spending the night, Camille and I drove another three the next day to see her father for a few hours, then we would return to my mother's house later that night. The visit was interesting and a little eye opening. He gave me my birthday present (my birthday was in the early part of December), this gift he kept forgetting to send to me, so I got that on Christmas Eve. It was a very beautiful watch and he gave me a small angel figurine to add to my collection that I had started. The price tag was still on the bottom, $4.95. Warning bells started going off in my head that day. He had brought Camille a wind suit that was beautiful but too small, so we took it back to the store and she picked out a blazer that she liked and he also gave her some money. Him being who he is, sensed that I was dissatisfied with the small gift that he gave me; brought me a pair of leather gloves that was on sale. The purchase of the gloves made me feel a little better but not much. We spent the rest of the day with him and his family and then drove home to Mom's house very tired from our long day.

He and Little Davie came to see me for the weekend in early spring. Alana spent the weekend with my sister in Charlotte and Stephen spent the weekend with his friends from our old neighborhood. I wished that he could have left Davie so we could really be alone; I did make arrangements for my children, and the least he could have done was the same for his son. He did have a sister, daughter and niece that were quite capable of keeping him. We had been alone only once since we got back together, after that it was, "Let's wait until Davie goes to sleep then we can sleep together, you lay in one bed and I will lay down with him until he goes to sleep." What kind of stuff is this, are we basing our time together on a little three-year-old? Him being a three-year-old and a smart one at that would pull the old "can't hang can ya" trick on the two of us. He would stay up half the night and David said that he didn't have the heart to spank him or make him go to sleep. When he finally did go to sleep, we would make love very quietly, as not to wake Davie, then he would climb back over in the bed with his son..

We had a nice visit that weekend with little Davie under foot all the way, then it was over and he was gone. After that, the phone calls dropped off to a couple a month and the mail was practically nonexistent. I started getting lonely and angry; it didn't seem as if he was making any plans to do anything about us really being together. After a while, all his words were being repeated when I did hear from him.

"Be patient…someday…you know I love you…I'm sorry I didn't write you back, but I was thinking about you"

"David, I'm getting really lonely and I have started to go out with my new girlfriend Charlotte. We have been going out to this jazz club every weekend and when I see couples out together, it makes me lonely for some companionship," I would tell him whenever we got the chance to talk.

"I didn't say that you couldn't go out, that's fine, but please try to stay strong until we can be together."

"You need to communicate with me more, even if it is just a small note once a week, that's all I need. But not hearing from you is killing me and I'm telling you that I am getting very weak."

"Very weak?" he asked.

"Yes, very, very weak," I replied earnestly. And I was. I had met Charlotte through one of Alana's new friends at the apartment complex that we lived in. We hit it off right away and started hanging out together. I started noticing men looking at me. I had lost weight and I was looking pretty good. I didn't want to start looking back at these men, but sometimes, I did. It had been such a long time since I had enjoyed the company of a man. David was so far away and didn't seem too interested in nurturing our long-distance relationship. I was getting lonely, wanting to be with him, but not being able to. I started feeling as if he had left the survival of our relationship up to me.

I started getting lunch invitations from guys at work. Most of these men were much younger than me. Two in particular were in their late twenties. I went out with them on occasion, but I just couldn't get into younger men. One in particular was shy and very intimidated by me; we went out to lunch one day and he ordered all this food and couldn't even eat it and he didn't look up at me not one time during our meal, or I should say my meal. I tried to carry the conversation, but to no avail. The other young man was a lot of fun; we became good friends and he made me laugh all the time. But, there was no chemistry there as far as I was concerned. He liked me a lot and was actually very old beyond his years, but I really didn't like him in the way he liked me. We still remained friends until he moved to another city and then we lost contact.

My next venture was a guy I met one night at a jazz club; he was the waiter. Every time I would go to the club, he would come by and talk to Charlotte and me. He seemed like a really cool person and as if he was really attracted to me. I was flattered more than being attracted to him; it was very obvious to me that I needed some practice at this single thing. I felt like a lost sheep going out and not really knowing how to conduct myself when men came around. He started to really come on to me one night, and I hadn't heard from David in a couple of weeks, so I started flirting with him. His name was Richard. I told him that I was involved in a long-distance relationship. He said that was fine with him, that he just wanted to get to know me. I wasn't dumb enough to think that was all he wanted, but this man intrigued me. He was not an unattractive person at all, I liked the way he carried himself and he seemed very attentive. He started calling me a lot and we would talk on the phone—nothing heavy, just small talk really. Charlotte convinced me to invite him over for dinner.

"I don't know, maybe I shouldn't. I've never done anything like that before." But; the more I thought about it, the more exciting it sounded. No, I had never done anything like that before but I decided that I would start. Here I had my own place and I was sort of unattached. Besides, it was only a dinner, that's all.

I was determined to keep this just an everyday plain old dinner between two potential friends. I had cooked spaghetti and garlic bread and made a garden salad. I was running behind the evening he was to come over, so Charlotte came by to help me.

"I brought a few things for your table. I hope you don't mind," she said. She began setting the table with this very beautiful dinnerware. She always had a romantic flair about herself and after she finished setting my table, it looked as if I had romance in mind for the evening.

I looked at the table after she finished setting it. "Charlotte, don't you think the candles are a bit too much? I don't want him to get the wrong idea!"

"It looks nice, Carol. Besides, you need a little romance every now and then. Call me later and fill me in. Bye," and then she was gone. I really didn't want him to get the wrong idea; yet, in a way I did so I left the table set as it was.

The evening went by smoothly and after dinner, we sat on my sofa and watched some television. He was holding my hand. I should not have let him do that, but it felt good having a man touch me again, even if it was only to hold my hand. Before I knew it we were kissing and boy could he was a good kisser! Things started getting pretty heated between the two of us. I decided to try to change the mood; I got up from the couch and started for the kitchen, just trying to get away from those all too familiar feelings starting to build up in my body. Once I got in the kitchen I turned to find him right behind me. He reached for me around my waist and gently leaned me against the wall and began kissing me.

"I haven't been able to think about anything but you all day. I want to make love to you." Oh how wonderful those words sounded to me, especially since it had been a while since I had heard from David. At first, all I wanted to do was to have him to make love to me, but I wasn't ready for that.

"No, I don't think that would be a good idea, my kids are due back any minute now." Good excuse, now if they would only burst in the front door, I would not have to find another reason to say no. I moved out from the embrace we were in and walked shaken over to the kitchen counter and reached for the pitcher of tea I had prepared.

"Richard, would you like another glass of tea?" I could not look at him as I asked that question, afraid that I would see such passion in his face that I would melt and fall into his arms and eventually end up in bed with him. Before he could answer, my son came home and not too long after that, my daughter. When he left later that night, he gave me such a kiss that I almost wished we had made love earlier.

Six o'clock the next morning, the phone rang; it was him. We talked for a little while, then I got ready for work. As soon as I got to work, he called me again. He called at least two more times that day and now all of a sudden, he is in love. I picked up the phone and dialed. "Charlotte, he told me that he was in love. Now how could that be?"

"Carol, you'd better get rid of him and fast, he seems too clingy already and he hasn't known you that long."

"He even wants to start bonding with Alana, says he loves kids, and wants to take her to the movies. What would I look like letting a stranger take my daughter to the movies? To top everything else off, I believe he is married. Just a feeling, but I'm sure he said something about his wife one time, during a conversation we had."

"Think of something, girl, but I don't have a good feeling about him. If you don't get rid of him now, you might have a hard time later."

The next day, when he called first thing in the morning, I told him that I didn't think it would be a good idea for us to see each other.

"Are you married?" I asked him.

"Well, sort of, but we don't get along too well."

"I don't think we should see each other anymore, it wouldn't be a good idea."

"Alright" was all he said and that was that. I just stood there, a little shocked. That was easy, I thought, I hope that will be the last time I hear from him, and it was.

I felt a little guilty about "going out on David" but he was not making any effort at all towards our relationship. I called him one evening after not hearing anything from him in weeks. "Why haven't you called me or written me? I'm here waiting and waiting to hear from you and nothing, nothing at all, David."

"Carol, why is it that every time we talk, it's about the same thing?"

"Because, I'm wondering if you really want this anymore, I'm wondering if you really want to make an effort towards being with me. It doesn't seem as if you do, David."

"Why don't you get a divorce first, then we will talk."

I could tell he was angry; well, so was I, so I hung up on him; I thought he would call back, but he didn't.

Chapter 25

It was getting close to the holidays; Thanksgiving was just around the corner. I'm sure he was waiting for me to visit my mother for Thanksgiving or at least Christmas. This would make it easier for us to see each other, especially if I did all the driving, but not this time or ever again. I decided to stay home for Thanksgiving, and I hadn't decided anything about Christmas yet.

That last conversation with him started me to thinking about our entire relationship and about how much I didn't know about him. There was a part of him that was emerging that made me feel that, perhaps he really didn't want to marry me. Did I once more try to create or control a situation in my life that I wanted? Was I forcing things to happen the way I wanted them to? This question I was not ready to answer; I didn't want to think that he didn't want me after all we had been through. That thought hurt real bad. I decided not to call him, to wait for him to call me, just back off for a while.

Meanwhile, Charlotte and I continued to go out. We found this new place to go to; it was shortly after Thanksgiving. I remember the night quite well; it was very cold and the atmosphere in this club was really kind of cool and cozy. It reminded me of one of those very small smoky clubs you see on television with a small stage surrounded by cocktail tables and chairs. Not a very large place at all; there was something about it that made me want to stay there all night. We had a few drinks between the two of us and just milled around listening to the band.

There was no place to sit so we just stood around and tried to stay out of the way of the front door. It was constantly opening with people going in and out. The air was very cold and I tried to stay away from the front door as much as possible.

At one time, I had moved around the bar by a window that faced the patio of the club. The patio was used during warmer weather for the overspill of patrons. As I looked out of the window, I saw a tall, dark and handsome man wearing a long black cashmere coat pass by the window. I remember thinking how interesting he looked. He was so handsome, very chiseled face and his skin was dark and smooth; he didn't look like any of the locals I was used to seeing in town. As soon as he entered the club, he disappeared into the crowd. I didn't give him much thought until later that night; I was standing by the inner wall of the place lost in a song that was being played. I can't even remember what song it was, perhaps "Stormy Monday," I don't know. That's when I heard this deep voice behind me say, "You seem to know something about that song." I looked around and it was the tall, dark stranger I had seen enter the club earlier.

He looked even better up close. I remember thinking *Why is he talking to me? He's a little too good-looking; I'm not even going to fool with him.* I don't know how I responded to his comment. All I know is he was trying to have a conversation with me and I was trying to move away from him. When I excused myself, I found Charlotte and told her about him. "I'm not talking to him, I don't want to get into any trouble with that man, but he is fine!"

The night was wearing on and people began to leave. We seized a table with four chairs immediately. A couple came in and joined us at our table, we began talking and introducing ourselves, then the table next to ours became available. My tall dark stranger decided to take a seat at the next table, and wouldn't you know it, he was aquatinted with the couple at our table. So there we all were talking and listening to the good music when all of a sudden I heard from the other table, "Let's go out on a date. I'll take you out and we can have fun."

What do I say now? I asked myself. "I'm sorry but I'm engaged," I said.

He still tried to hold a conversation with me. He asked me all sorts of questions like "Where is your fiancé? When are you going to be married?"

I explained that he lived in another state and that we had not set a date. I was hoping that he didn't try to look at my finger for signs of an engagement ring. All the time I was telling him this, I felt as if I was lying to him and myself. Finally, Charlotte and I decided to leave, we said goodbye to everyone and my tall stranger rose to his feet and wished me "good luck," then we left.

My birthday, number forty-four, was coming up in the next few weeks. Charlotte and I planned to celebrate at the jazz club. Meanwhile, I had not heard from David, nothing at all from him. I was starting to hurt inside, started to realize that perhaps he and I were not "meant to be," that even though I had prayed for us to be together, that God had other plans.

One night, Charlotte came to see me and found me in tears. David had not called so I decided to finally call him and we argued about the same thing. It seemed as if that was all we did whenever we did talk.

"Every time I hear from you it's the same questions over and over again, Carol—when will we see each other again, why haven't I heard from you?" He sounded very frustrated with me.

"I'm not spending any more money on us; I'm not running my phone bill up anymore." I felt that now was the time for him to start working; if he wanted me, he had to come to me. That part of me that would do anything to be with him had died; that death felt good. I felt a little empowered as I hung up, yet I was still hurt, I wanted us to be together so bad.

"Carol, don't cry, it'll be all right. Your birthday is soon and we are going to have a real good time. Maybe that guy will be at the club and we can all celebrate together."

"You know, Charlotte, you're right, we are going to have some fun and we will celebrate—it's my birthday!"

"I'll go over to where he works and see if he will come for your birthday. He works at that electronic store up the street doesn't he?" she asked.

"I think so. Let me check—he gave me his business card." I went and looked in my purse and got out the card he gave me. Yes, he did work just down the street from where I lived.

"Charlotte, go see if he will be at the club on my birthday. I feel like exploring this guy. Who knows what will happen?"

We had run into him the week before at the club and the three of us had a good time. I found out that his name was Dallas. We talked and he told me he was in sales and gave me his business card with his home phone number on the back of it.

I decided that on my birthday, I was going to start to look towards my future; wherever that road would lead me, I was going with a newfound attitude. I was slowly but surely coming to the realization that David may not be in my future, at least not the way I had envisioned it. But that was all right with me; perhaps the experience with him was, as everything is in life, a growing process. Even though I received a birthday card from him that said "Happy Birthday to my Wife" and on the inside, he had written "soon," I didn't believe that any longer and I accepted it. I started to feel something well up inside of me and that something is still growing; that something is self-love, the greatest love of all. So, on to the future and it will be a future full of bumps and curves, but one where I can face and love myself for myself and know that I can stand alone, but not really alone; I know I have God on my side.

About the Author

I was born in the coal fields of Bluefield, West Virginia. Later my family moved to the town of Huntington, West Virginia, where I grew up. I was a member of the first all-girls track team in high school in 1970–1971. After graduating from high school, I married and moved to Fort Walton Beach, Florida, then Atlanta, Georgia, and have lived in Winston Salem, North Carolina for the past twenty years. I guess you can say I'm a southern girl. I have worked in the office arena all my life from file clerk to accounting, payroll and credit. I have three grown children and four grandchildren. I enjoy writing, singing, gardening and especially cooking. I have even dabbled in the food arena for a while running my own catering business. My greatest accomplishment, however, was raising my children.